PRAISE FOR

Waiting for a Star to Fall

BY KERRY CLARE

"Kerry Clare's *Waiting for a Star to Fall* is a love story at its core, though one without an ending written in the stars. It's about what we believe—and *who* we believe—and it reveals that we each control our own happiness and destiny. Timely and insightful, Clare has crafted a worthy successor to her memorable debut *Mitzi Bytes*."

—Karma Brown, #1 bestselling author of *Recipe for a Perfect Wife*

"Kerry Clare has done something spectacular: She's written a riveting #MeToo novel that is a nuanced celebration of the complexity of human nature. I read it in one morning and will be thinking about it for a long time to come."

—Lauren Mechling, author of *How Could She*

"Girl falls hard for charismatic, older man. It's heady and intoxicating. Then he turns out not to be who she thought he was. Like, at all. This is a thrillingly sexy book about that first big, bad love, and the pain of seeing someone for who they really are. Kerry Clare writes about the dark heart of women with a deceptively light touch, one that belies a complexity just below the surface. A diverting and compassionate read." —Lisa Gabriele, author of *The Winters*

"Timely and entertaining on the surface—but crack through to its core and discover a deep and thought-provoking meditation on the flaws and foibles of humanity. This book is beautifully, brutally honest, reminded me of being 23, made me forgive myself my lapses in judgment—and, made me long for whatever Kerry Clare will write next. Fans of Emily Giffin and Curtis Sittenfeld take note: This is your next read."

—Marissa Stapley, bestselling author of *The Last Resort*

"A skillfully told story for our times, *Waiting for a Star to Fall* takes readers on an emotional journey. Clare's expert handling of this all-too-familiar yet difficult subject is sure to spark meaningful book club discussions."

—Chantel Guertin, author of the Pippa Greene novels

"When Kerry Clare's *Waiting for a Star to Fall* landed on my desk, I could not restrain myself and read the entire novel that same day. Taking a now familiar story as her starting point—famous man pummeled by sexual assault allegations—she ventures beyond the headlines, into terrain news stories can't cover. What gives these mediocre men their outsized confidence? Why do they act with so little regard for others and how do they keep getting away with it? Searching for answers, Clare turns the spotlight on her women characters, the ones who are hurt by these men even as they continue to enable them. A deft examination of power, complicity, and accountability, *Waiting for a Star to Fall* is thoroughly engrossing. Clever and insightful, this book is a sheer delight."

—Sharon Bala, author of *The Boat People*

"I'm in awe of Kerry Clare's tender, imaginative care for the characters in *Waiting for a Star to Fall*. I was right there with them, viscerally in the moment with all their best and worst ideas, especially with Brooke, hoping for what she hoped for even when I worried about the outcome. Such a fully realized, fascinating, enthralling world Clare has created—I was completely enraptured."

—Rebecca Rosenblum, author of *So Much Love*

"*Waiting for a Star to Fall* is the novel we need at this moment: a wonderfully sharp and humane examination of power and betrayal, love and limits. Kerry Clare has told one woman's story, but many of us will recognize ourselves in this rich portrait."

—Elizabeth Renzetti, *Globe and Mail* columnist and author of *Shrewed*

Waiting for a Star to Fall

Waiting for a Star to Fall

A NOVEL

KERRY CLARE

DOUBLEDAY CANADA

Doubleday Canada and colophon are registered trademarks of Penguin Random House Canada Limited

Library and Archives Canada Cataloguing in Publication

Title: Waiting for a star to fall / Kerry Clare.
Names: Clare, Kerry, 1979- author.
Identifiers: Canadiana (print) 20200241052 | Canadiana (ebook) 20200241060 |
    ISBN 9780385695473 (softcover) | ISBN 9780385695480 (EPUB)
Classification: LCC PS8605.L3605 W35 2020 | DDC C813/.6—dc23

Cover design: Terri Nimmo
Cover image: Galina Kamenskaya/Getty Images
Cover art (interior): Talia Abramson

Printed in Canada

Published in Canada by Doubleday Canada,
a division of Penguin Random House Canada Limited

www.penguinrandomhouse.ca

10 9 8 7 6 5 4 3 2 1

This book is for every woman who was ever 23.

"MURDOCH CRUISES TO AN EASY WIN"

SO LET'S CALL IT a comeback. Seven months after resigning as party leader due to allegations of sexual misconduct, hometown boy Derek Murdoch cruised to an easy win in the mayoral race, defeating four-term incumbent Caroline Rawlings in a surprise upset. Defying pollsters—not for the first time—and delivering a swift jab to opponents all too ready after the scandal to declare Murdoch finished in the world of politics, he would stand up in his victory speech and declare himself vindicated.

"I want to thank my family, and the people of Lanark for always standing by me. The last few months have been a journey," he said, "but everything that's happened has only made me a stronger person, a better politician. My friends, this is only the beginning . . ."

Seven Months Previous

Tuesday Morning

She hadn't been drinking—this was the thing. Yet that morning Brooke woke up with a hangover, and it took about five seconds to put the night back together again. She had a different taste in her mouth, but the weight on her head was just the same. So what had happened? What had led to the restless, uneasy sleep that she was now shaking off like a blanket, eyes struggling to come to terms with the daylight?

And then there it was, reality settling over her like dread, and it was all coming back: the press conference, watching the live-stream as her phone buzzed. A bombshell that ricocheted, the whole thing unfolding with no warning of what might happen next—except Brooke had some guesses. A level of insight into the general narrative that didn't serve to make her feel better, or wiser. It made her feel worse, and she'd broken out in a sweat, even though her extremities were freezing and her legs were shaking the way they'd been shaking the second time—which was really the first time—that Derek Murdoch kissed her.

It was uncharacteristic, that's what they all said. The pundits, and the people online who were paid to talk even when they didn't know what they were talking about. They explained how Derek wasn't a person who ran away from challenges, no matter how difficult. *Principled.* That's what they kept calling him, the key to his character, they supposed. They'd never seen him like this, so rattled, and Brooke would admit—as she'd watched him falling apart on the screen—that she hadn't recognized him either. Could the breakdown be part of a performance? Was this the strategy they had in mind? Maybe it was supposed to be humanizing. Because she couldn't think of any other reason for Derek to have fared so poorly. Professionally, at least, he'd never been unprepared for anything in his life.

When the whole thing started kicking off, Brooke was miles and worlds away from the action. She was babysitting—a part-time gig she'd found after tearing a phone number off a poster on the community board at the library. The poster belonged to Marianna Tavares, a single mom who worked at a seniors' home, mostly day shifts, but she needed someone to watch her daughter on the odd evening. An arrangement that worked fine most of the time (the one upside of no longer having a social life was availability for odd jobs to supplement Brooke's meager income), but what an odd evening this one turned out to be, Olivia finally tucked into her bed upstairs, asleep. Brooke was scrolling on her phone, thinking about putting on Netflix, when she received a text from her sister Nicole, the first time she'd heard from her in ages: *What is going on NOW?*

Brooke replied with a string of question marks—and then her phone buzzed again. And again, and again. She hadn't taken Derek's name off her news alerts when she left his office, and now his name was everywhere. There had been allegations, two women saying shocking things, and he'd be holding a press conference, pre-empting the story before it broke on the newscast at ten o'clock.

Everything was happening on Twitter, and Brooke scrolled through her feed, ignoring her sister's message, searching for some confirmation herself, an understanding of the bigger picture, but she could find none. Her desperation for clarity mingling with fear, frustration, even fury. *What have you done?* she was thinking. After all she had given him—and forgiven him—over the course of his career, and hers—to have it all come down like this. Was there no limit to how much Derek could betray her?

As she refreshed her screen again, new details appearing, they finally began to form a picture. And it was also a relief to realize this was not one particular shocking story it could have been, blowing up her whole life all over again, only this time with the world watching. This breaking story now had nothing to do with her—although this also underlined how remote she had become from Derek these last few months. Entirely out of reach—and yet, not so far that she couldn't discern what was going on. For years, shady characters had been willing to offer to pay for dirt on Derek, something to mess with his image, to tarnish his sterling reputation. Brooke had seen them sniffing around, had even talked to some of them directly, and now, apparently, someone had finally taken them up on the offer.

Derek would have known this too, which was surely the reason he'd been so indignant as he stood before the reporters, sending the press conference off the rails before it even began. Where he should have been calm and assured, he was agitated and angry, and not remotely convincing as an innocent man as he pledged to push back against the allegations. He was going to fight to clear his name, he explained. Except he hadn't been in fighting form at all, particularly at the end, when he'd been speaking through tears, and then he'd cut the whole thing off abruptly, reporters chasing him down three flights of stairs.

Marianna was home by then, and she and Brooke were watching the whole thing together, and witnessing Derek in this state—he was so pathetic, with the crying and the running away—seemed to snuff out any residual anger Brooke had been harboring toward him these last few months. She had been imagining him back in the city, living his life as though nothing had happened, while her whole world had ended, and she'd let herself yearn for a sign that he'd suffered at all. A self-centered twist on empathy, for him to know what she knew, what she felt, and she'd wondered whether it might even feel good to see him hurting—some kind of justice delivered, his comeuppance. But now she knew that it didn't, not at all, because it felt so unnatural not to be on his side, and because whatever else Derek had done, he was paying for it now—that much was obvious.

Marianna proclaimed the whole affair "a gong show," and Brooke couldn't argue. Derek's performance had been so bizarre, the allegations so tawdry. And why did he have to fall apart like that in front of the cameras? Running scared. The one detail she kept getting stuck on, because it just didn't make sense. The Derek she knew would never have let that happen. Was no one looking out for him?

Marianna wanted Brooke to stay, she'd open a bottle of wine the way they had on other evenings, and together they'd hash the whole thing out—she hadn't sat down in front of the TV news for years, she said, it was kind of fun. Trying to decipher the puzzle of baffling men was one of Marianna's favorite pastimes, although she'd never once gotten to the bottom of it. But what Marianna didn't know was that Brooke had a personal investment in the matter unfolding on TV before them now, in this particular baffling man, and Brooke didn't want to get into it with anybody, let alone somebody who wasn't even properly a friend. The emotions were still too raw for her to be detached enough from any of it, and nobody she'd tried to explain her connection to Derek to had ever understood.

She walked home from Marianna's with her phone in her hand, still buzzing. She should have turned off her Derek alerts months ago, but they had been a useful way to keep track of him, to have him be part of her life, however tangentially. She'd received a message from her mother: *What is happening? Are you okay?* A sinking feeling as she read it, because of how much her mother didn't know, the dark places her imagination might take her.

Which was why she called Nicole, who picked up right away, saying, "This is insane."

"Hello to you too," said Brooke.

"Did you know this was coming?" Nicole asked.

"I don't know anything anymore," said Brooke. "I was babysitting."

"You saw the press conference?"

"I saw it."

"He cried."

"Well, people do." Brooke was not going to defend him, even though Nicole was waiting for her to. It was truly a reflex she really had to fight—for five years it had literally been Brooke's job to put the many sides of Derek together into a comprehensible and sympathetic story. But now she wasn't going to do it, give Nicole the satisfaction.

Nicole was waiting. "It didn't look good."

"Not at all," said Brooke. "Listen, I need you to call Mom. Just let her know that I'm all right. That I know as much about all of this as the rest of you do."

"You're really okay?" asked Nicole. She knew Brooke too well, which had made her hard to be around these last few months, or even to talk to, Brooke preferring the company of a near-stranger like Marianna. Or even no one. Because the last thing Brooke wanted to do was stare her truth in the face, to have to listen to her sister spell out the reality of her situation—that she was truly broken and still hung up on a guy who'd left her stranded. But for tonight, at least, Nicole would be able to help Brooke avoid a conversation with her mother—Brooke was up for that even less.

"Listen, I'm nearly home," Brooke said in lieu of an answer to the matter of her well-being. Home now was a basement apartment in a triplex whose weedy lawn she was traversing. The faint cellphone signal underground was always a good excuse to escape these conversational traps. "If you could call her, I'd owe you big time."

"Of course you would," said Nicole. "But any thoughts of paying me back soon? I want to see you."

"Sure, sure," said Brooke. "Maybe sometime in the next few weeks."

"Which is what you've said any time I've talked to you in the last few weeks."

"I've been busy."

"Busy avoiding me."

"I'm not," said Brooke. "There's just a lot right now. And then tonight—"

"I'll call Mom," said Nicole. "But you have to let me take you out for dinner."

"In the next few—"

"—weeks. Yep, I know," said Nicole. "Listen, you take care of yourself, okay? And if you need anything, you always, *always* can call me."

Brooke told her sister, "I know."

For the last few months, since her sudden return to Lanark, Brooke had mainly been successful at keeping the feelings at bay, as well as the people who'd force her to feel them. Although, she had always been a bit like this, and it had become her defining trait, her levelheadedness. The way she did not give in to emotions, to their powerful draw, but instead stuck to facts and worked her way through them. She could be a hero in a crisis, adept at strategy. The sensible one. She could rise above the morass and look down below, figuring a way to get through it, instead of succumbing to the panic. No, she would not panic, it was not her style—but surely now she'd reached the point where she could finally declare *enough*. Thinking of everything that had been heaped upon her these last few months, and now this: the allegations and the press conference. Her headache compounded by the force of it, her heart like a drum. She didn't need it spelled out, really, how alone she was here, and she'd done that to herself. Except he'd done it to her first, leaving her in this desperate place, and there was no one she could tell the story to, because they'd only hate him. They'd misunderstand, or they would understand too well—and which one was it? But now it seemed like everybody hated him anyway. This cause she'd been fighting for all these months was a lost one, and even thinking about it felt like drowning. She had to get up now, or else she'd never be able to get up at all.

Now fully awake and all too steeped in the facts of the night before, Brooke hauled herself out of her bed, which was just a mattress on the floor, and rolled into the kitchen, where Lauren was sitting at the table eating toast, scrolling through her phone. This was one thing about Lauren that

Brooke hadn't appreciated properly until this moment: she thought celebrity gossip constituted "the news," which would serve Brooke well today. Plus, she made great coffee, and now gestured for Brooke to help herself. But all the mugs in the cupboard were ugly, Brooke despaired, and none of them were hers.

"Are you okay?" Lauren asked, Brooke presuming she looked as terrible as she felt, and she asked Lauren if she had painkillers. Her head ached even more now that she was upright. Lauren had a bottle of ibuprofen in the cupboard, alongside all those jars of her boyfriend's supplements and vitamins, and Brooke gulped two down with coffee in a mug with a gas station logo. And then she went back to her room to get dressed, ignoring her phone, or trying to. Determined not to check it, because once she started scrolling, there'd be no end to that, and in the meantime she'd have to head into work like this day was ordinary. This crisis was not one in which she was immediately affected, as difficult as that was for Brooke to get her head around.

Because before, of course, this crisis would have touched everything. As one of the longest-serving members of Derek's staff, she would have been alerted right away, been part of an emergency task force to help get ahead of the story before it was all over the news. It was the rush she loved, even in the most impossible challenges, the kind of work that got the blood going, enough adrenaline that everybody could forget that they hadn't slept in twenty-four hours. Ordering pizza and guzzling energy drinks, or else something stronger. Whatever it took to stay above water, drafting statements and trying out various defenses.

This whole thing was obviously a setup. The allegations in this case were both more than a decade old, which certainly did help his side. There'd be no evidence of anything anyway, so why had those women waited so long to come forward? It was political opportunism, part of a conspiracy, and Derek's name had been besmirched. Damage done. *Besmirched.* Such a funny, old-fashioned word. What even was smirching? There was a musty kind of morality to all of this, Brooke knew, and it could be spun.

If she had been there last night, would things have been different? Would Derek still have broken down and cried, running away from the reporters? If she had been there, maybe he would have been stronger. He wouldn't have run away, a coward. The pieces were already shattered, and he'd made everything worse, possibly unsalvageable. As though every step down those three flights had further ground the fragments under his feet, and how do you put that back together again? His staff would be doing their best, she knew. It's what they were there for. If she had been there, she would have promised him that everything would turn out fine.

But making promises to Derek wasn't her job now, professionally or emotionally, and she was only spinning in her mind. The reason for her headache, she supposed, because she couldn't relax or think of anything else. She showered and got dressed, headed off to work, taking the bus because of a chance of rain, but this was a mistake because she was so jittery, her legs bouncing up and down. The woman sitting beside her with a bouquet of shopping bags noticed and was trying to move over, to put more space between them, but there wasn't much to go around. So Brooke got off two stops early, figuring a walk would do her good.

She checked her phone now, finally—just to see the time, but also all the notifications. The messages the night before from her sister, her mother, but that was it for actual people. None of her former colleagues had been in touch— but why would they be? When she'd been shuffled out of that office in shame back in June, Brooke had mostly ceased to exist as far as they were concerned, and all her years spent cloistered in that political bubble had long ago cut her off from everybody else. Although the isolation she had come to appreciate, one bit of a silver lining to being trapped here in this no-man's land, because she couldn't imagine how she'd explain it, what might happen if she had to account for herself. Mortifying. So angry and heartsick, and she'd sound like a fool. Everybody would know that she was one.

What a mess it all was, she thought, scrolling right down to the end of her notifications, the initial alert that had started it all: *BREAKING: Murdoch holding late-night emergency press conference.*

She cleared her phone now, blanket deletions. It was noise, all of it, a story still developing, too soon for conclusions, and all those assholes who'd seen it coming: "I never trusted the guy." Never mind that they had been bending over backwards to stay in that guy's good books, to get him onside so they could get him to do their bidding. Everybody was a special interest group—but not Brooke. She was a rare breed in politics, she knew—she'd learned from the best.

Though she had always been like this. A reliable and diligent teenager, Brooke had been appointed to the school board as a student representative, where she discovered that behind the scenes was where the real work happened, unlike the popularity contest that was high school politics, which was mostly about organizing spirit rallies before the football game. It was the kind of showmanship she'd never gone in for, preferring substance instead, and Brooke had learned that much of what people recognize as politics— ideology, dogma, ego, spin—was really a distraction. What mattered was facts, and truth, and the weight of people's stories, and when you really took the time to listen, walls came down and the space between didn't seem so wide after all. Politics worked when you took the politicking out of it, which is what Derek had always told her, what they'd both learned from their years in the trenches.

And for sure, there were those who indulged in practices that gave politics its bad reputation, the power-grabs, lying, cronyism and chicanery—because that was the way it had always been done. But Brooke knew there was another way. Faith was fundamental to her politics—not the religious kind of faith, but instead certainty that there really were things to believe in. This was what had drawn her to Derek in the first place, the way he affirmed her ideals about how the world worked and what it could be. It was where they had always seen eye to eye.

When Brooke arrived for her shift at the library that morning, however, and began her first task—the newspapers—that long-held certainty was challenged. Unrolling the day's editions—the increasingly diminished national papers, all three of them, plus the local daily and the weekly—pulling each one apart section by section, then reassembling them on wooden rods designed for optimum organization and easy reading. Before any of this, however, she had to remove yesterday's, folding each paper back into a tidy stack. Yesterday's papers didn't know about any of this, their headlines still screaming about electricity rates, and Derek would be quoted somewhere in the article, common sense, the voice of reason.

But today he was on every front page, photos from that moment at the press conference when he'd started to cry. Looking guilty as anything, it could not be denied. How could you spin a face like that?

The headlines today all-caps and all-incriminating:

DEREK MURDOCH ACCUSED OF SEXUAL MISCONDUCT

BEFORE

The first time Brooke met Derek, she was downtown at Slappin' Nellie's, a dive bar Derek's best friend Brent Ames had bought up and resurrected a few years before as part of a wider effort to rejuvenate the downtown core. It was the go-to place, where they were lax with ID if you didn't make a point of being conspicuously drunken. And staying under the radar was fine with Brooke, because the whole scene was overwhelming—dark walls and flashing lights, pumping bass and dancing bodies—and she was uncomfortable with the idea of being absorbed into it. Instead, that night, she was watching, swaying, smiling, because she'd had two drinks, but there would be no more. She didn't want to lose what little cool she had, ending up like her friend Vanessa who, at that instant, was vomiting into a toilet already stopped up with reams of paper towel.

Because as much as Slappin' Nellie's was their current stand-in for something worldly, being here only underlined to Brooke how much she wanted more than what this place had on offer. She knew that at the end of the summer, she and Vanessa would go their separate ways, and it was the possibility of it all that had Brooke swaying with more verve than usual that night, feeling above her station, perhaps, when Derek Murdoch appeared at her side. Scoping out the scene himself as he sipped his drink, offering a conspiratorial glance. He was better-looking than in photographs, she noted. Before, Brooke had wondered what his appeal really was, but seeing him in person, you could almost understand.

"Your friends are out there?" he asked her, gesturing toward the dance floor, and Brooke nodded, even though they weren't. She didn't want to let on that she was alone. Derek said, "Well, then, why aren't you dancing with everyone else?" That old song was playing about the bed that's on fire with passionate love.

But Brooke was determined not to be undone by his charm. She shrugged. "I don't have to dance with everyone else."

Derek nodded intently, like he was really considering what she'd said. "What's your name?" he asked. "I think I've seen you around."

"I've never been here before."

"Around town, I mean." They had to shout to be heard over the music's crescendo. "You look familiar."

She said, "Do I?"

"I'm Derek," he said, as though he were offering her something, as though everybody didn't know his name already. As though Brooke hadn't seen his face on election signs all over town just a few months ago. He'd been a city councilor in the municipal election before that, the youngest person ever to be elected to office in Lanark, and she knew the whole Fire Boy Hero story. She also knew, like everybody else downtown did, about his reputation with the ladies. He "liked to have a good time with them" was perhaps the genteel way of putting it.

It was a reputation Brooke was pretty sure was not unfounded, especially with the way he'd sidled up beside her . . . but now Derek was pointing across the room at the guy in the DJ booth, Brent, almost as much of a local hero as he was. Derek said, "Listen, you know my buddy, Brent? He owns this place." Brooke nodded. He said, "He'd get in a lot of trouble, see? If cops found out there were high school kids here."

Brooke waited a moment. "What are you trying to say?"

"Just watching out for my friend," said Derek.

"Okay," said Brooke, drawing out the word with a sigh. Derek Murdoch wasn't just a dork, he was an asshole. Who did he think he was, the liquor control board? The youngest person ever to be appointed to that too, no doubt.

"What *is* your name?" he asked, just before she walked away from him.

She said, "I'm Brooke."

"Hi, Brooke," he said, extending his hand now, like this was an election and he was installing a lawn sign. If she'd had a baby, he would have kissed it. Derek Murdoch was a cheesy guy, but his schtick was less off-putting than it should have been. He was watching out for his friend, his business. She'd been expecting sleaze, but he'd turned out to be more upstanding, even if it was annoying, and maybe the rumors about him were wrong, was what she was thinking as she accepted his handshake. As he leaned in close and confided, "You're right, you know. You don't have to dance with everyone else." And then walked off into the night.

The whole encounter had been dazzling—or maybe that was just the lights and the booze, or that he was this famous guy who'd picked her out of a crowd. Whatever it was, after the fact, she had a difficult time believing that any of it had really happened.

Which was the reason she hoped she would see him again, and she did, nearly half a year later. By this time she had been away at school in the city for an entire semester, but was home for Christmas, out with a few high school friends who were turning into strangers, and once again she felt apart from things, standing at a remove.

Then there he was, alone. She recognized his profile, and approached him without even deciding she would. And was this that thing called charisma, such an inexplicable draw? She'd only ever read about it in books before.

Once she'd come up beside him at the bar, he turned her way. "You're Brooke," he said. And so the draw was explicable after all; he'd remembered her name. *This* guy. Who was waiting now with an expectant look—like he knew she'd be impressed. And she was. But did remembering her name mean that she was special or that he was, with such a remarkable skill for recognition? Either way, she liked it, but she didn't want to show how much.

"We've met before," he reminded her.

"I know," she said, "but I'm not in high school anymore, so you don't need to worry."

"I'm not worried," he said. "But listen, I know you. I do. It's driving me crazy. I've seen you before, I'm sure of it, but I just can't figure out from where."

"You mean, apart from the time you threatened to have me thrown out of this place?"

"It wasn't like that. And you're just so familiar."

She said, "Well, you're kind of familiar too." Playing like this was a two-way street, catching him off guard in the process. And surely he would call her bluff? But then, what kind of a person would he be if he did? Only the kind of person who is aware of just how important he is—but Derek Murdoch didn't want to give that impression. He tried to wear his power like a shrug. "Where do I know *you* from?" she asked him. Like a joke.

He said, "Well, I work in politics." He didn't get it.

"Politics?"

"Party stuff, elections, making laws. You know."

"I know about politics," Brooke said. The music was quieter up at the bar than where they'd spoken the last time, beside the dance floor. She didn't have to shout for him to hear her, and suddenly she felt a desire for him to know they had a connection after all. "I study politics," she told him. "At school in the city."

"Oh yeah?"

She said, "And I'm kidding, of course. About not know-ing who you are. I would have voted for you. If I'd been old enough then." She sensed an ease come over him with this statement, a return to familiar ground.

He said, "You mean that?" And from his expression, she could tell it was important that she did. That he needed her to, that he even desired her approval. And because she really did mean it, she told him so, and then he bought her a shot. "I mean, since you're not in high school anymore." Now he was the one teasing.

He gave her his card. "For when you're back in the city," he said. "And even when you're not, I mean. We're always looking for people who are into politics. Lots of ways to work together. Email me." She tucked his card into her tiny purse and returned to her friends feeling a little buoyant, light-headed, or maybe she'd just had too many drinks. Her euphoria abated somewhat moments later when she saw Derek on the dance floor kissing a blonde girl, his hands all over her body.

Tuesday Afternoon

What if she just skipped today? Brooke considered as she dealt with the newspapers in the library. What if she just left the newspaper rods empty? "It's not like there isn't plenty of other stuff to read in the library," she would explain to anyone who complained, and the only people who came in to read the papers were old people anyway. Everybody else read their news online now—although she could put a stop to that too if she switched off the power bar at the computer bank and disabled the Wi-Fi for the people who read the news on their phones. "The whole system's gone down," she'd say if they asked, feigning sheepishness. "Too bad, too, because I've got absolutely no idea who's being accused of sexual misconduct today. But what are you going to do?"

And if her best friend Carly were there, she'd be rolling her eyes, bursting out in frustration, "Why are you always defending him? Protecting him?" She'd be asking why Brooke was always making excuses, discovering loopholes, fixing it all, concocting fabulous explanations for why Derek's behavior was just fine. For sure, if Brooke had been there at the press conference the night before, she would have been the one waiting downstairs in the parking garage with the ignition on, the getaway car. Roaring around sharp corners at top speed, just to get Derek out of trouble—but it was here that her fantasy was extinguished. Derek never let her drive. It was always him behind the wheel.

She felt the same instinct, though, to shield him, to excuse him. And not just because all that had been her job for so long. The single reason Brooke was grateful Carly was far away right now, doing an internship in South America, was that she wouldn't have to explain to her friend what was really happening in her life, what was happening to Derek. Because if she did try to explain, Carly would only dismiss the fact that this was a setup, character assassination, sheer political opportunism.

"But do the details even matter?" Carly would demand. "If everything they're saying, in general, is basically true?"

Can you really convict a man on the basis of his poor character though? Could that be enough? Wasn't it the facts that were supposed to count, facts Brooke could hardly believe herself as she skimmed the papers below the head-lines to understand? These women who'd come forward were being used by Derek's foes both inside and outside the party. They were pawns, their stories batted around for political gain, accusing Derek of such terrible things.

The Derek they were describing wasn't the person that Brooke knew, and even if the last few months had suggested that Brooke didn't know him so well, she didn't want to see him suffer. Another fact, but one that would have Carly demanding: *Why not?* Because wouldn't it be a kind of restitution? Maybe, but there was nothing satisfying about it, and Brooke would continue to insist Derek was a better man than Carly thought he was, because what would it say about Brooke if he wasn't?

Skipping the papers, however, would be futile. And her task was to keep her head down, perform her duties and not make waves, because she needed this job and her life didn't need any more upsets. She had to resist the urge to make the library a small island of calm in the raging sea that was today's breaking news. The waves would overrun the banks eventually. She didn't have the power to shape how the story would go.

So the papers got hung, albeit with the front section turned around backwards so there were car ads facing out instead of headlines in all-caps. But it didn't even matter, because when Brooke returned to the circulation desk, she found her colleague Lindsay involved in an intense discussion of those headlines with Sheila, the chief librarian. The two of them nattering on like this was gossip, something salacious, and Brooke wanted to duck right back out again, but Lindsay spotted her, inviting her to join in: "Have you heard? Murdoch's finally getting what's been coming."

It was too late to run. Brooke asked her, "How do you know? That he's had it coming?"

Lindsay said, "Well, why else would his staff quit?"

"Who?"

"Everyone. Chief of staff, the press secretary, all the others."

This was news. That everyone would jump ship at such a pivotal moment. What was the point of a team if they didn't stick by you? How had everything gone so terribly wrong?

Sheila added, "And he's still refusing to resign."

Brooke couldn't make sense of it. Last night at the press conference, Derek had vehemently denied everything. "Anyone who knows me—they know that I would never be capable of the things that I've been accused of. It's not the kind of person I am. Those of you who know me—you know. I know you do." It was the best part of his performance, his voice steady and strong, his eyes staring straight into the camera, into the eyes of the public.

But then he cried and ran, and if his entire team had quit overnight, this did not bode well. And Brooke knew how all of this would have come about—Derek's chief of staff was Marijke Holloway, who'd supported Joan Dunn in the leadership race, and years later, resentment from that contest remained. Derek had brought Marijke on board to bring more experience to his team, though he'd been advised that it was a naïve and stupid move. He'd done a poor job smoothing things over, and Brooke knew Marijke would be looking for any excuse to betray him. It was the nature of the game.

So who had been with him last night? she wondered. If the team had handed in their resignation, who'd been there to sit up for the pizza and the strategy? After that shameful exit, down three flights of stairs. Had he gotten into his car alone?

Lindsay said, "How the mighty have fallen. He's going to have to go." For her, this was something to celebrate. Another predatory male down for the count, and she just assumed that Brooke would feel the same. If it had been anybody else, Brooke probably would have.

But now she said, "Not necessarily." It was the fiercest opposition she could manage while retaining her composure.

Lindsay said, "Huh?" She was emptying the returns bin, and the scanner wouldn't work. She slapped it three times against the desk.

Brooke didn't want to engage. Nothing about this was anything to celebrate, but then Sheila stepped in to save her, an unlikely ally, unafraid of asserting her point of view, because as chief librarian, it was her prerogative.

"Well, it's not really fair, is it?" Sheila challenged. "Two anonymous accusations, and it's all over? Do you really want a system that works like that? What if it was you? That could be my son. Next time, it could be yours." Employing all the usual clichés, Brooke noted, wondering if it was impossible to have a conversation about any of this that wasn't idiotic.

"But it wouldn't be my son," Lindsay said, "because I'd never have a son like that. And it's not just two. You know it's not just two." Where there's smoke, there's fire. "There's a pattern here. He's being accused of inappropriate relationships with young girls who work for him. Anyone disputing that?"

"But they're not young girls," said Brooke. "They're women." Lindsay was changing the details of the story to suit her agenda. Brooke picked up the books that were being checked in and filed them on the cart.

"They were teenagers." Lindsay was insistent, and disappointed that Brooke was letting her down, onside with the boomer.

But Brooke was on a roll now. "Ten years ago," she reminded Lindsay.

Sheila said, "And it's not illegal, any of that. Those two accusations aren't about relationships; they're saying he *raped* them. Or that he nearly did—but where do you draw the line? And they've got no proof. Why would they wait so long to come forward?"

Because there was an election coming up in the spring, Brooke knew, but what she said was, "We're talking about grown-up people making their own choices. Those women knew what they were doing."

"Oh, honey," said Lindsay, and that was the limit. Brooke was fine with disagreement—anyone who'd worked in politics had to be. But being patronized was something she was unwilling to put up with. Lindsay said, "You think a twenty-three-year-old woman knows what she's doing?"

"I'm twenty-three," Brooke said.

And Lindsay replied, "That's what I'm saying."

———

Brooke went down into the stacks and hung out in Natural History, around a corner so remote that no one ever went there. Here she could finally click on the story, the one Derek's press conference had tried and failed to pre-empt. She'd managed to avoid the details so far, preferring to glean what she could from the headlines, Twitter threads, gossip and hearsay. From skimming. On the one hand, she'd told herself, she didn't even have to read the story, because she'd been in the business long enough—the business of politics, if not the business of Derek—that the story would only follow a template she knew well. In a day or two, as they say, the whole thing would blow over. But on the other hand—the hand she'd never show, and even had trouble admitting to herself, because it was the truth of the matter—maybe she didn't want to know, out of fear the story might turn out to be something different altogether.

But it was time now, because Lindsay and Sheila had caught her off guard. There wasn't a template for what was currently unfolding, at least one that wasn't terrible and torn from the pages of a supermarket tabloid, and everything was changing so fast. This wasn't blowing over. Pulling out her phone, typing into Google, there it was:

TWO WOMEN ACCUSE MURDOCH OF SEXUAL
MISCONDUCT

Who were these two women? It was possible she'd met them both—politics was as small as Lanark was—but then, ten years ago was an eternity, and most of the people she knew hadn't been around back then. Not women, certainly, who tended to burn out on the long hours, low pay, and the realization that it would be their male colleagues who were promoted and moved up through the ranks. Each one hoped that she might be the rare exception, not merely one of the others. But of course, they all were the others, and there had been so many of them, women who, like the two in the article, had met Derek back home in a bar downtown and gone on to work for him. Not a lot had changed, and the stories were familiar, even though Derek had worked in municipal politics back then.

So it could have been anybody—this was the thing. Speaking of templates.

Derek always said it was "HR expediency," the way he reached out through his social networks, recruiting staff from a dive bar. People would call him on it, and he'd try to explain, saying, "I don't know a better place to find young, dynamic people who are looking for their first jobs, for summer jobs." Derek had a talent for making anything he thought up seem entirely reasonable, mostly because he really tended to mean what he said.

But reading the details made her feel sick to her stomach, and she sank from her squat against the bookshelf, dissolving onto the dusty floor.

"I told him to stop," one of the women was quoted in the article as saying a decade on from the alleged incident, which had begun at one of his parties. She'd had too much to drink, and he'd taken her keys away from her, offering her a place to stay in his spare room. That sounded like

Derek. But then. Later that night the woman awoke from her stupor to find him with her in bed without any pants on, attempting to penetrate her, and he wouldn't listen to her protests. "I tried to get him to stop, but he ignored me. It was almost like I wasn't even there, except as a body. That was all I was to him."

Was she even capable of presuming the truth of this woman's story? Brooke asked herself. She knew that Derek had been with other women before her—he was so much older than she was. He came with a history, and she couldn't hold that against him. But she had never liked to think about that history too much, certainly not in this kind of detail. Could he really have done something like the article said? She could even picture the room where it had been said to happen. Whose side was she on?

The woman continued to work for Derek for another year, the article reported, in summer and between her terms at college. She accompanied him on business trips. Their relationship became intimate. Which didn't help the woman's case, Brooke thought.

"But it wasn't like I got over it," she said in the article. "It wasn't even that I put it aside or forgot, but instead I pursued our relationship. I wanted it to happen, because if we were together, I thought it would make what happened that night all seem okay. But it was never okay. It just took me a long time to realize how wrong it was."

The second story was even harder to fathom, and reading it made Brooke feel even sicker. This woman had been at Slappin' Nellie's with Derek, and he'd tried to force her to give him a blowjob out back, behind the patio, where the garbage cans were. "He had me pinned against the wall," she said, "and I kept trying to get away but I couldn't. He kept pressing his erection against my leg, and he undid his pants. I honestly thought he wasn't going to let me go unless I did it." He eventually relented, but she was still traumatized, the woman said. "Nothing like that had ever happened to me before. It's just not the kind of thing that normal people do. He was like an animal." This woman, at least, had not agreed to travel with him to Barcelona after the fact, and she only worked for him for the rest of the summer. But still.

The original article from the night before had been updated to include details of the mass resignation. "I cannot in good conscience continue to support this man," Marijke Holloway had written to the press in an email. "It's a time for all of us to stand with survivors. Our party needs to do better."

Which sounded noble, but wasn't the whole story, because Marijke had never properly stood with Derek anyway, and Brooke knew she didn't have his interests at heart. It disgusted her, too, the way that these women's stories were being used and manipulated so that somebody out there—a whole bunch of somebodies, Marijke Holloway among them—could score a few cheap political points. So that people like Sheila could have their opinions on the matter, asking just what exactly *had* that girl been doing with Derek out by the garbage cans at Slappin' Nellie's? Was out by the garbage cans even an actual location? Brooke couldn't visualize it, but it sounded sordid. Hearing a voice that sounded like Sheila's in her mind: *And what did someone imagine was going to happen in a place like that?* And Brooke knew that if everyone listened to voices like Sheila's, no man would ever have to be responsible for anything.

What if it was me? Brooke considered. That person whose personal life had just turned into a political weapon? Lindsay didn't have it right either. None of this was really about justice, or even about protecting women. There'd inevitably be holes in both women's stories, and soon everybody would be calling them liars, which was why you don't take meetings with low-lifes offering you money for your story from that time you got too drunk a decade ago. Because once the story isn't yours anymore, no amount of money could possibly be worth it.

She read the article right to the end. It was awful. Then she sent Derek a text, the first message she'd sent him in a while, breaking a silent streak of more than a month, which had been so hard-won, but now everything was different. *Just thinking of you. I'm here if you need to talk, or more.* Derek's whole world had fallen to pieces, and maybe nobody else had thought to check in and see if he was okay. Really all she was saying was, "You are not alone," and then she texted that message too, just to be clear about it. Waiting a moment for him to reply, the familiar vibration of her phone. There had been a time when the buzz between them had been constant. Derek would make a speech that would be the top story trending that night, and three minutes before—from where she was waiting, ready to watch him go live—she'd receive his message: *You're my good-luck charm*. Sometimes totally out of the blue: *You're amazing*.

But her phone was still and silent now, the way her heart felt, slumped down there on the floor. And she imagined him feeling the same, all alone in his room, those empty walls a void. She sent him one more text, the same thing he used to say to her: *You're amazing*. She'd texted him too many times now, but these weren't ordinary circumstances. If Derek was as desperate as he seemed, a bit of support could make all the difference in the world.

Which was the trouble, of course, how everyone these days came down so hard on others for all their faults and frailties, forgetting that these people being held to such exacting standards were only human. Humans whose faults and frailties were magnified and compounded under media scrutiny, along with the pain and vulnerability that might have caused the faults and frailties in the first place. Though, Derek's was a problem that was partially of his own making—he always had to insist on being more than only human, which establishes an impossible expectation for a person to have to live up to. Was it only inevitable that it would all fall apart?

Brooke went back upstairs to Circulation, where Lindsay apologized when she saw her. "I wasn't being flippant," she said, "but I know the fire these women are going to come under. I feel for them."

"I feel for everyone," said Brooke, and Lindsay started telling her a story about an old boss who'd once tried to kiss her in an elevator. "I had no recourse," Lindsay was saying. "It was literally part of my job description, putting up with that shit."

"Well, that's not right," said Brooke.

"For me, I guess," said Lindsay, "the whole thing is a little bit personal. I'm thinking about those girls. I've *been* those girls."

But people ought to be able to be responsible for their own choices, was what Brooke was thinking. If Lindsay's old boss had made her uncomfortable, surely she could have taken the stairs? Even though it made Brooke ashamed to think such things, and she knew she sounded like Sheila, which was opposed to all her politics. But if people weren't responsible, see, it only meant that you were not in charge of your own life, and who would ever want to believe such a thing about themselves? To accept this, Brooke thought, felt like a surrender, a life sentence. But she said nothing about these complicated and blasphemous thoughts to Lindsay, instead nodding and going about her duties refreshing the stack of date-due slips as her co-worker continued to explain that these poor girls were victims, that all of us girls were victims. And then Lindsay left for the reading room to take her turn at the reference desk, leaving Brooke to climb up into the chair at Circulation, adjusting it accordingly, holding the lever so the seat rose—Lindsay was very tall.

Brooke was still fiddling with the backrest when she heard a voice she immediately recognized, and she contemplated adjusting the chair so it would sink so low that she might disappear behind the counter. But it was too late now. She'd already been spotted.

"Jacqui Whynacht!" she exclaimed, like this was good news. Run-ins with people like Jacqui Whynacht are the reason most people tend to flee their hometowns at the first opportunity.

Jacqui flashed a ring, informing Brooke, "It's Jacqui Diamond now." Evidently she'd married her high school boyfriend Matt, or else his brother, because you never know in Lanark. Her hair was blonder, and she seemed shorter, or maybe just weighted down by the toddler on her back. "When did you get back to town?"

"Beginning of the summer," Brooke told her, taking the books that Jacqui unpacked from a cloth bag, *Good Night, Good Night, Construction Site* the one on top. Brooke pretended to examine the titles carefully, anything to divert attention away from herself. Jacqui had always been intense. She'd run the morning announcements in high school, her shrill voice ringing through the hallways and classrooms with way too much enthusiasm. Brooke had never understood what Jacqui was so excited about, and even now, she felt herself wilting in her presence.

"Where are you living?" Jacqui asked, fishing for something in her enormous duffle bag. "Are you back home? You got a place yet?"

"A place?"

"A house," she said, still rummaging. "It's a buyer's market, you know. It's not going to get any better than this." Finally Jacqui had it: her card. She laid it on the counter before Brooke. "Diamond Realty," she said. "Family company. Lanark's top-rated—you've probably seen the ads on benches."

"I'm not really looking," Brooke told her. "I'm just renting right now, temporarily. I'm sort of in-between—"

"In this market?" Jacqui was shaking her head. "You're throwing money down the drain."

"Well, I don't know what my plans are," said Brooke. "I'm still just kind of taking stock."

"Setting up a meeting would be a good start," said Jacqui, gesturing toward her card on the counter. "Listen, do you have a card?" She looked around for a pile on the desk, but Brooke didn't have that kind of job, nothing business card–worthy. "Why don't you give me your number," Jacqui said. "I'll keep you in mind, let you know if something comes up. Ow, Jared." The kid on her back was pulling her hair. She said, "I've got to get him to the babysitter. Here." She plucked a brochure of library programs from the pile on the counter. "Write your number here. Maybe we can get together? Have coffee."

"Looks like you're pretty busy," said Brooke.

"I could swing it," said Jacqui. "It's great you're back. You were down in the city, right? Before? You're not on Facebook, are you?" Brooke was on Facebook, but her account was hidden, except to a handful of close family and friends. Jacqui said, "There's this group for young women, professionals. I could add you. For networking."

"I'll give you my number," said Brooke. Maybe a little networking wouldn't be so bad. So she wrote it down, with her email, pushed the brochure back, and Jacqui stuffed it into her crowded bag. Her kid was really squawking now, pulling on her hair again, and Jacqui rolled her eyes playfully, like this was adorable. Brooke knew only a few people her age who were having kids already, and this was her first instance of seeing it in real life. To be honest, it just looked cumbersome. Marianna, whose daughter she babysat, was perpetually exhausted.

"I'll be in touch," said Jacqui. "And keep my card around. You never know." Prying her son's fingers out of her hair again. "Good to see you!" she called out over her shoulder as she hurried out into the world.

An hour later, Lindsay came back to the circulation desk, and Brooke went to straighten the periodicals, which were mostly as straight as they'd been first thing that morning. Someone had taken down the day's papers but, instead of reading them, they'd fallen asleep under them as though the papers were a tent. The sleeping man was a regular—Brooke recognized his boots—and one of the blessed few who didn't snore. As she walked past him, she checked out the headlines again, the paper rising and falling gently with each of the man's breaths.

When Morgan arrived for the afternoon shift, Lindsay and Brooke got to take their lunches—a half hour each, one after the other. Brooke hadn't brought anything to eat that day, having been lacking in both time and groceries, but after four months at the library, she'd learned there would always be leftover cake in the staff room. This one, with gaudy blue frosting, was from the birthday celebration of one of the women who worked in the Tourist Information Bureau—they shared the library building, along with the Downtown Business Improvement Association—and it was only vaguely stale. Brooke slapped two slices on a plate and then stretched out on the couch to eat them, the plate balanced on her chest as she scrolled on her phone. If anyone was coming, she'd hear them on the stairs with enough time to sit up and look civilized.

Derek hadn't replied to her texts. She thought of reaching out again, just in case her other texts had been lost in all the hubbub since the story broke, but she wisely resisted the urge. She had sent him three texts in five minutes, and she regretted it now. There were no circumstances in the world under which that would seem cool.

But Derek probably wasn't thinking about her at all, she knew, so instead she used this time to get caught up on the latest. Nothing had been released since the memos of his team's resignation, the party trying to act as though it hadn't just been sunk by a torpedo, and that everybody wasn't headed for the lifeboats. "Our party is not just about one man," someone was saying, as though the situation was still salvageable. "We were a party before Derek Murdoch, and we'll still be a party after he's gone." Having finished the cake, Brooke felt a bit ill, but blue icing will do that. She thought about how willing the party had been to make it all about one man back when it seemed that man could deliver an election victory. Derek's face was everywhere, huge and imposing, on billboards, pamphlets, internet ads. There was relief in the prospect of not having to stare into his eyes all the time, and everywhere, that face she knew so well, and loved, but in images so bland and unseeing.

This was the story she'd been telling herself, and to anybody who asked: the library was a good place to work—there was no overtime, the tasks were not exacting, and it gave her the same experience of public service she'd enjoyed in her last job. It was a similar opportunity to effect change, to make a difference in people's lives—except now she was being trained on how to deliver naloxone to prevent overdose deaths of vulnerable patrons, and helping new immigrants format their resumes, plus making conversation with frazzled new mothers whose trips to the library saved them from isolation. And there were books, which had once been such an important part of Brooke's life—her mother had taught high school English and was an avid reader, recommending title after title to her daughter, the downside of this being that Brooke had never learned how to discover books on her own. And then, when Brooke went away to school and got so busy with work, she became estranged from books altogether. She'd fallen out of the habit of reading, and didn't understand how to fit books back into her life, so now she appreciated her encounters with them here at work, accepting returns, shelving those copies, retrieving others, rearranging the out-of-order titles so that the next person who needed a book would be able to find it. In politics, she'd discovered that so few systems worked—but libraries did. The world was not yet wholly bereft of things to believe in.

But this was still a demotion, the end of a career path that had led nowhere. Her skills and experience didn't count here, and maybe they never would again, never mind the humiliation of returning home to Lanark cloaked in a shame she could not delineate to Jacqui Whynacht, or anyone. "It was time for a change," she'd explained to her family and to her friends, but ever so vaguely. Everyone waiting for her to properly account for her situation, but she couldn't, she wouldn't, not when she was still waiting to see what might happen next, because there had to be a resolution. And in the meantime, she was waiting, seemingly endlessly some days. The pace at the library could be so slow, she missed the adrenaline rush, and nobody ever went out for drinks after work. The job wasn't fun, not the way that politics had been fun, and the stakes weren't as high—but at least it was meaningful. And it was better than working in an open-plan office with meetings all day long, somebody always looking over her shoulder, no place to hide. It was better than having no job at all. Brooke had been counting her blessings, even though by the time her four o'clock home-time came around, she'd been waiting forever, and she'd have to go through the whole routine again tomorrow.

But before tomorrow, she headed down the street to Jake's Pizzeria, whose proprietor was her father, who'd inherited the business from his father (neither one of them called Jake), and where she'd worked as a waitress all through high school, which is where Derek Murdoch had known her from before he knew her name. To lots of people in town, Brooke was "that girl from the pizza place," cute enough with a swinging ponytail, but part of the scenery, basically. She'd served Derek several times throughout her teenage years, but he had never paid her any special attention until that night at Nellie's—but she'd always been able to count on him for a decent tip.

The restaurant was deserted tonight, maybe because of the drizzle, but it was also early. Brooke's dad was wiping down the counter. He said, "I wasn't expecting you."

"One great thing about having a daughter who has no friends left," said Brooke. "You get to see me all the time."

He said, "You've got friends."

And she let him think so, because it made him feel better. Back in the city, all the people she'd once called friends had forgotten her, and up here there was Jacqui Whynacht. "Let's just say I've got room in my calendar."

"Your mom's been texting you," said her dad. "How did it go today?"

"At the library?"

"With Derek and the news." Brooke's parents adored Derek, the way everybody in their town did, and once she'd gone to work for him, it had become personal, their feelings about Derek a reflection of their love for their daughter.

43

"I guess everyone's seen it," said Brooke.

Her dad said, "He never should have let you leave there." Her dad was a famous overestimator of Brooke's talents and was convinced she'd been the brains in the whole Murdoch operation. "If you'd been there, you might have given better direction. Like telling him not to start crying. Did you see that? Did you see the way he ran away?"

"Three flights of stairs," said Brooke. Professionally speaking, she would not have made any difference, not to the optics at least. She had good ideas, but nobody was obligated to listen, and her relationship with Derek usually meant they made a special effort not to.

Her dad said, "Babe, I'm sorry."

"For what?"

"For you, for him. I don't even know." Her dad threw the cloth in the sink. "I read the story," he said. "What those women are saying—you don't know anything about that, right? I mean, he was never like that with you?"

"Oh, gross, Dad." Brooke was peering into the cabinet to see which slices were out under the heat lamp. As far as her parents were concerned, Derek had been like her big brother, the family forever in his debt for the opportunity he'd given Brooke in her career. They didn't know that he'd met her downtown at Slappin' Nellie's. And if they'd heard the rumors, they never mentioned it. Brooke said, "It's all a hit job. Don't even think about those stories." This was her father; she couldn't have him thinking about those stories. She nodded at the pizza in the display case. "These are fresh?"

"Of course they're fresh," said her dad. Brooke gave him a look. "No, really." Public health was really laying into local restaurants—just another example of the government interfering in people's personal business, her dad would complain. Some people liked buying a slice of pizza that had been sitting out so long the cheese had turned to rubber.

About Derek, her dad said, "You really didn't see this coming?"

"I did and I didn't," said Brooke. She slapped the cheese slice onto a paper plate and packed a pile of napkins beneath to soak up the grease. "I'm really out of touch up here."

"You haven't talked to him?"

"He's busy," she said. "Damage control."

A group of customers came in, and the evening waitress wasn't in yet, so her dad showed the group to their booth, Brooke sitting at the counter, eating slowly, savoring the texture of the stringy cheese. Even hours old, her father's pizza was delicious. The twenty-four-hour news channel was playing on the TV on the wall, and there he was again, Derek, tears in his eyes, ducking from the microphones and running away. One last shot of the stairwell, and the back of his head, and Brooke wondered again where he'd been running to. Down the corridor was the entrance to the parking garage—she could draw a map on the back of a napkin. She hoped the sprint had paid off, and that Derek had made it out into the night with nobody on his tail. Heading home, maybe, back to the safe haven of his condo a few blocks away.

At Derek's condo, all the shelves were bare and there was nothing on the walls, the place barely lived in, which used to make Brooke feel like part of the couple in the photo that comes with the frame. Wall-to-wall white carpet, marred only by a red-wine stain from where she'd tipped her glass one night when they were up late arguing about religion. That was the kind of thing they'd talked about, the conversations she'd been missing all these months. Like no one else she'd ever met, Derek had ideas, and he relished the opportunity to be challenged on them. That night, she'd been saying that Jesus was alienating in a secular world, while Derek maintained he was still an inspiring teacher, and his insistence was infuriating. His composure turned her into the emotional one. Made her start waving her hands, too emphatic, knocking her glass off the coffee table, and the lush white carpet soaked the red up.

In the end, the only answer was to move a chair over the spot, but the stain was there, and Brooke knew it still bothered him. That night was the first time she'd ever seen him lose his cool—he liked to be able to fix things, but the stain was indelible. She'd tried to assure him that it really wasn't such a big deal, but everything—her voice, her touch—just made him angry, so she shut right up. There are tricks for getting wine out of carpets, and he was looking them up online as the stain got deeper, and at least they knew not to touch it, not to rub it in. But the tricks required items like salt or baking soda from the kitchen, and Derek's cupboards, as usual, were empty, save for wet-naps and ketchup packets. They'd only ever had takeout at his place, Brooke remembered now, picking up her napkin and dabbing at her mouth.

"Murdoch hasn't made a statement since his dramatic exit at last night's press conference," said the television anchor. "Since then, his entire staff have resigned."

Her dad was back by her side, staring up at the screen. "You think he really did it?" he asked. "All those things they said?"

"Of course not," Brooke told him, hoping she sounded sure. But now Blaine McNaughton, Derek's political nemesis, was on the screen. "It's an open secret," he said. "We've all been hearing the rumors for years."

"About sexual assault?" asked the reporter.

McNaughton shrugged. "It's a slippery slope," he said. "I mean, everyone knew about Derek and girls. And how far it went? I don't know. But it's a question of character. In politics, you've got to demonstrate that you're deserving of trust, and your reputation is all you've got. He should have been more careful."

"He's vowing to clear his name," said the reporter. "Do you think there's any chance of that?"

McNaughton was shaking his head. "Listen, I like the guy," he was saying. "I've known him forever. But this is not going to end well. I think it's probably time to move on."

"THE DEREK MURDOCH STORY"

UNTIL THE AGE OF ELEVEN, Derek Murdoch was an average kid, eldest son of Jim, a janitor at Lanark Town Hall—"Cleaning up politics is in my genes," Murdoch quips—and Ann, a medical receptionist and local dynamo, who not only coached her son's hockey teams, but also played the organ at St. Stephens church on Sundays. A series of photos shows the family over the years on the steps of St. Stephens, a mid-century modern building all angel-stone and sweeping peaks, a sleek white cross in front. First Jim and Ann in their wedding attire, and then each new addition—Derek, his sisters Tracey and Heather, and brother Carl—the children each two years apart, posed in a row, tall-to-small, heads like stair-steps.

"We were a working-class family," Derek likes to remind people, harkening back to his humble origins even though his early politics were different from those he espouses today.

In the 1980s, Jim Murdoch led efforts to disband the Town of Lanark's employee union, whose leadership he viewed as corrupt and against workers' interests. His campaign failed, but many have argued that the union has been powerless ever since. Meanwhile, Jim went on to become involved in local politics, working for candidates who shared his own priorities of fiscal restraint and family values. It was a road his son might have followed him on, but for the harrowing events of April 29, 1990.

His mother still can't talk about it, and leaves the room when Derek tells the story. It had been one of those summer-like days in April with a clear sky, not a cloud in it. He and his siblings had been playing in the backyard of their modest bungalow. "It was warm enough to be wearing just a light jacket," recalls Derek. They were running in and out of the garage, which was usually out of bounds, but somehow the door had been left unlocked. Ann was in the house, so she didn't see what her children were up to, and even now no one knows for sure what happened next.

"I heard a bang," says Derek. He thinks it was probably a gas tank, which they kept in the garage for filling the mower. There were other chemicals too, and maybe one of the kids was playing with matches. "But who was doing what exactly doesn't matter," Derek emphasizes. "I heard this noise and realized they were in there, my brother, and my sisters. And I could see flames through the window." Ann had sewn eyelet curtains for the window in the garage, same as the curtains in the kitchen, and after the fire she had to get rid of those ones, too painful a reminder. "The curtains were on fire, and I remember the way they just burned and fell away like ash," he says. "And I was scared, but I also knew what I had to do. Everything was in slow motion, and when I touched the doorknob, it was already hot."

Derek went into the garage, and now shrugs off any suggestion that his action was courageous—"It wasn't a choice," he said. "Anyone would have done what I did."

The next part of the story is told from patched-together recollections. His mother came out to see the garage in flames, Derek emerging from the inferno with her daughters in his arms. And then he went back in to get Carl, only four years old at the time, who hadn't understood what was happening and had been hiding, afraid he'd get into trouble.

There were stories in the local paper the next day, and in the national papers the day after that: "Fire Boy Hero Saves His Siblings." This was the first time a photograph of the family on the steps of St. Stephens would appear in the press, a photograph taken just two weeks before, at Easter, Derek looking hearty and strong, ruddy-cheeked, having nearly outgrown his blue suit jacket whose sleeves don't meet his wrists. By the time his image was all over the wires, Derek had been transferred to the largest burn unit in the region.

Ann returns for this part of the story, because she knows it best. She spent the next year at Derek's hospital bedside, advocating for his care, while Jim and the church community held down the fort at home.

"He'd suffered burns to 40 percent of his body," Ann explains. "The skin grafts were agonizing and seeing him like that—I thought at that time—would be the worst thing I'd ever experience."

"It changed everything," says Derek. "I mean, it changed my life, our family, it changed the way I'll always look. But most important, it changed the way I see the world, because it made me realize: What are we here for, if not to take care of each other?" He's not just talking about his heroic action, but he also means the firefighters who responded to the call, the care he received in the hospital, the medical staff who, he says, "went beyond the call of duty," and the community fundraisers—car washes, bake sales, and a benefit concert—that raised thousands of dollars to support the family.

"Society is all we have," says Derek. "And those of us who can, have an obligation to lift each other up." It's an idealism at odds with the individualism that had been his father's political foundation, which has certainly led to rifts over the years, slamming doors and emotional spats, but that's standard for any family with teenagers.

Jim explains, "I'm proud of him. I am. I don't agree with everything he says, and I think the world is going to teach him a lesson or two, but I really do see him as a testament to our family's values. He goes out into the world and does good. He chooses to do that. Nobody makes him."

"And after what happened to me—the mercy and the blessings I received," says Derek, "how could I not want to pay that back?" As a teenager, he started working with the church youth group, doing outreach to the city's poor and downtrodden, helping to establish addiction counseling services, an employment assistance program, a co-op day care, and a food bank with a cooperative garden and nutrition programs. Derek was leading the group in 1997 when they came under fire by the church for their work on sexual health programs, which were seen as promoting promiscuity and being contrary to religious doctrine.

"It was awful," said Derek. "St. Stephens was my home. My parents were married there. It's where I was baptized. They were my family, my community. But they were asking me to compromise on something I knew in my heart was true, and people would suffer if I followed their advice. I couldn't abide by that."

"We're proud of him," Ann says. "Like his dad says, we don't agree on everything. I don't think we ought to be giving kids license to be sexually active. That's not how I was raised. That's not how we raised our own kids. But I know that what Derek's doing comes from the very best place. It's a real kind of faith, what he's got, really, to think we can get along in a world without rules."

"We've learned," adds Jim, with a chuckle, "that there's no telling Derek what to do."

Derek ultimately left St. Stephens, but continued his work in social justice.

"My faith is important to me," Derek says. "My parents instilled that, and it's never faltered. But I needed to be part of a community whose mission was to bring hope to the hopeless, health to the sick, and food to the poor. To not let dogma keep us from seizing every opportunity to do good."

It was a difficult period for the family. "Derek leaving the church was a loss," says Ann. "St. Stephens was our center, and when one of us isn't there anymore, the center is broken. That was really hard to deal with."

At the same time, their youngest son Carl was experiencing his own challenges, eventually seeking solace in drugs and alcohol. "It was like he became a different person," Jim says. "Overnight, really."

"He was my baby," says Ann. "My sweet baby boy—and then suddenly he was a stranger, and it was like living with a time bomb—you never knew what was going to set him off."

"And we just weren't equipped to handle it," said Jim. "Used all the tools in the toolbox, you know. At the church, at school. He was in rehab. It cost a fortune."

"It was Derek who never gave up," explains Ann. "Helped the rest of us keep going, like somebody who sets the pace. I don't know where we'd be today without him."

Carl passed away at the age of 17, when Derek was in his second year of law school.

"And he put the whole thing on hold," says Jim, tearing up. "He came back here, and he held us all together, and he made us go to church even though it was hard to find a reason. He made sure his sisters didn't have to pay a price, promised them that he'd be here to take care of us. And he did. He really did."

When Derek Murdoch blushes, the scars that have faded to become part of his healthy tanned complexion are more prominent, standing out in pink. He pats his father on the shoulder, and says, "You pick yourself up again. What else can you do? You've got to find the light." The family did this by establishing an annual fundraising drive for the rehabilitation center whose staff worked so hard to give Carl the support he'd needed. The Carl Murdoch Fund supports low-income families whose loved ones are battling addiction and who would otherwise be unable to access the programs that might save their lives, the programs the Murdochs had hoped might save their son.

"We re-mortgaged our house," remembers Ann. "And the church helped. St. Stephens was there when we, when Carl, needed them. And at least we have the peace of knowing we tried everything. I can't imagine the agony of parents who can't do that. No one should ever have to be put in that position."

This principle should not suggest that Derek Murdoch's parents have shifted their long-held perspectives on socialized healthcare, however. Jim says, "I've seen the bureaucracy firsthand, all the wait-lists and the red tape. It doesn't work. It's not the answer."

Derek blushing again, but this time with a smile. "But there's never just one answer," he says. "There's lots of answers, and expanding access to mental health ser-vices—more beds, more doctors—is a huge part of it. But also alleviating poverty, creating jobs and better support in schools, helping families in crisis. These are the tools for progress." He's got his arm around his father's shoul-ders now, each of them offering different solutions to the same puzzle.

Derek dismisses the idea that such family harmony is remarkable. "This is what family is," he says. "My parents gave me their values, but they also gave me the freedom to go into the world and make my own choices. Nothing was learned by rote in our home. All of it—the faith, commitment to service, the relationship with God—it had to mean something. Because if it doesn't, what's the point?"

Derek's sisters testify to him being "the best big brother ever."

"He took the load off the rest of us when Carl passed away," says Tracey, an elementary school teacher. "And he's been there for us ever since." Her sister, Heather, is a local real estate agent, and lives around the corner from her parents. Heather's three children love spending weekends with their uncle at his house in the country, just outside of Lanark.

Has his high profile changed things? The sisters laugh.

"We used to always go to the Santa Claus Parade," says Heather. "It was a really big deal, but Derek doesn't come with us anymore. He doesn't need to wait on the curb. Because he's in it. He's basically more important than Santa. They should probably change the name to the Derek Murdoch Parade."

"But he's the same guy he always was," Tracey explains. "He's had the same friends since he was in school, and they all still go out together like they always did, before the politics happened. He still likes to have fun. He's still my big brother."

Heather is nodding emphatically. "None of it has gone to his head."

This is his town, though, and when he walks down the street, people stop to say hello, and he asks them about their grandchildren, their kitchen renovations. When they want to talk to him about hip replacements and problems with hospital wait times, he listens attentively. He keeps a spiral notebook in his pocket where he writes things down, reminders. He wants to be accountable. He says, "I do my best to follow up on everything." And it's a commitment that's served him well in his work. The common perception is that Derek is not one of *those* politicians, the ones who are only in it for themselves.

"He's one of us," says Audrey Ames, who owns the Delicious Donuts store on River Street. "He's never forgotten where he came from. In fact, where he came from is the reason for everything. Nobody loves this town like Derek does. He really walks the walk."

Wednesday Morning

Brooke could have made things easier for herself—she could have just moved home. Her parents would have welcomed her, and her childhood bedroom had been preserved like it was a museum, her Obama "Yes We Can" poster still blue-tacked to the door—but that was the problem. To arrive back at the place she'd started from—the same floral comforter, too-flat pillow, tattered blinds—as though the past five years had never happened, nothing to show for it. So instead she went online and found listings for roommates, filtering out the college students because she was so over that, and ended up with Lauren, who worked at Jean Machine and whose fiancé was heading out west for a job in the oilfields.

Her apartment was one in a row of buildings Brooke had always seen from the car as a child, intrigued by the rows of gas meters and multiple doorbells at the entrance. What kind of people lived in houses like that? Everyone she knew lived in a proper house, with a big green lawn and a two-car garage. As Jacqui Whynacht had noted, Lanark was a buyer's market, and holing up in a rental unit was a last resort for the down and out. While Brooke wasn't there yet, buying a house required a commitment she wasn't willing to make, as well as money she didn't have. And of course it was scary, having all her pieces up in the air with no idea where they'd come down again—but she tried to take heart in the fact of still not knowing, in all the possibilities. Which was the way she attempted to tell herself that having had the world torn out from under her might prove edifying in the end—though in her darker moments she found the arguments unconvincing.

But the pieces in the air were the reason she now awoke to dim light from narrow rectangular windows tucked in just below the ceiling. When she forgot to close the curtains at night, she could see shoes and sandals passing by on the sidewalk in the morning, and the view was strangely compelling. Because where was everybody going? She'd gauge the weather by choices in footwear, since she couldn't see the sky.

Her room had been Lauren's boyfriend Jer's exercise room, and all his equipment was still there, pushed up against the wall. He'd only taken what he could pack in a bag, and so now Brooke used his bench press to hang her laundry to dry. And when the laundry was put away, there was no sign that anyone lived here, no photos or posters on display, not even a book by the bedside. She had brought nothing but the mattress. Just her phone plugged in, charging, charging.

She sat up and pushed the hair out of her face and checked the notifications on her phone. There he was, throwing her heartbeat into palpitations. At three o'clock in the morning, which would mean any number of things, he'd texted. *Hey B. Can't tell you what it means to have your support, but then you always know. Am lying low, but hoping to be home on Friday. Just what the doctor ordered, I suspect. x D.*

She began hauling herself out of bed. He was coming back. Not necessarily the best news from a strategic perspective, because shouldn't he be at work in the city, rescuing his reputation and clearing his name? If he was lying low, it indicated that he'd lost all hope. But even if Derek had lost hope, it would be good to have him close. This was the first she'd heard from him since July, and maybe it would be good for her if his mind wasn't on his job for once.

She went into the kitchen, where Lauren was drinking her coffee before her mid-morning shift. On the table in front of her, two pizza crusts on a plate. "Thanks for that." Brooke had brought home extra pizza the night before and left it in the fridge with a sticky note.

"You heard from Jer?" she asked. Lauren's boyfriend had been gone since his two weeks of leave back in August. Brooke had heard Lauren talking to him on the phone late into the night, her tone hostile and aggressive until he managed to talk her down and she started crying. The walls in this place were basically made of crepe paper.

Lauren said, "Finally." She'd been waiting three days for a call, and Jer hadn't been answering any of her texts. She was beginning to get worried—not even six months into a long-distance relationship, this didn't bode well. "His battery died. He lost his charger." She shrugged. "That's what he said."

"It sounds plausible," said Brooke. How easy was it to pop out for a phone charger in the middle of an oilfield? She was checking her own emails now, considering again what it meant that nobody she used to work with had bothered to reach out. Most of the messages in her inbox were, as usual, offers from brands whose newsletters she'd never signed up for, but there was one message that she clicked on. Shondra Decker, a reporter for the *Daily Observer*, wondering if Brooke would have a moment for a chat. *No comment*, she murmured to herself, and deleted the message. She asked Lauren, "So he's okay?"

Lauren said, "He's fine." She took one last gulp of her coffee. "It's just kind of hard?" Everything Lauren said sounded like a question.

And Brooke said, "I know." She did. Perhaps no one could understand how difficult the last twenty-four hours had been for Brooke better than Lauren, all these things happening to someone you love who's impossibly far away. In a cultural moment when all communication is so urgent and instantaneous, it only deepens the void when suddenly there's just none.

"I mean, it's not forever," said Lauren. "And if it's too hard, I can go out there, or he can come back. We've got it better than a lot of people, but I just want to make sure we're on the same wavelength about where we are, and where we're going. I thought we were, but now he's far away—how can you tell?"

Exactly. And Jer and Lauren had been together for years. So if Lauren didn't know where she was with her partner, what hope did Brooke have for getting her and Derek back on track? A question that recalled the words of her best friend Carly: "Lady, you're doing this to yourself."

BEFORE

Brooke kept Derek's card after their second encounter at
Slappin' Nellie's, and sent him an email once she was back
in the city. They were always looking for young people who
wanted to work in politics, he'd said, and Brooke needed a
job for the summer so she wouldn't end up back in Lanark,
slinging pizzas. Derek's assistant followed up on the applica-
tion, Brooke got an interview, and she was hired. She would
be working as a paid intern at his office, doing administra-
tive work and helping to manage volunteers, part of a team
performing supportive roles. It would also turn out to be the
best summer of her life. She'd already moved off campus
into the house she'd live in for the next four years, a place
shared with six other students and christened The Den of
Debauchery, although the name was purely aspirational.
Mostly, she just loved having her own room in the city, and

a job that didn't involve cooking grease. There were five of them in the team hired that summer, all of them girls who were young and pretty, with a bit of cultural diversity among them—Brooke and Nadia were white, but Kelly was Korean, Anjali's family background was Indian, and Eliza was Indigenous on her mother's side.

In the beginning, for Brooke, it had been like playing grown-ups, shopping for office attire, organizing the items on her desk, and practicing her best telephone voice—but then two things became quite clear. First, that there was no "playing" about it, because she was part of a team dealing with real people and real issues, and it was a real baptism by fire in the high stakes of politics. But the second thing was that because of the seriousness, a little "play" was more than necessary among the team, and so every night after work they'd all go out together. Very quickly Brooke felt close and bonded with these people, even the hardened veterans who had been at it for years, and such distinctions fell away during the time they all spent together. Soon Brooke's room-mates were wondering why they never saw her anymore, and her other friends were asking why she was avoiding them. Which she would have to reassure them about, she kept telling herself, as soon as she found the time to return her friends' calls. But there never managed to be enough time for that, and soon work and politics had become Brooke's entire world.

And it was a world that revolved around Derek, even when he wasn't there, and he wasn't there at all until her second week in the office. He had been away on a trip to

India in conjunction with the Board of Trade, and on his first day back, the difference in the office was palpable, the atmosphere buzzing, everyone speaking in voices slightly hushed and deferential, and Brooke would learn that no one dared profess their opinions on anything until the matter had been cleared with Derek first.

His office door was closed—he was notorious for coming in early, before anybody else—and he didn't emerge until halfway through the morning when his assistant, Petra, brought him around for introductions, to acquaint him with the pool of new girls who were going to be his for the summer. He singled Brooke right out of the crowd, giving her a hug. Brooke was the only one in the group who had met him before, which afforded her a kind of status among her colleagues. Later that day, over lunch out in the park, she would tell them all the story of their first encounter and how she thought he was going to have her thrown out of the bar. She liked the way her anecdote complicated everybody's idea of the kind of person Derek was, and suggested she knew him better than anyone.

When the work term started that May, Derek was in a relationship with a girlfriend back home, a woman called Miranda who was nearly as old as he was, which made it easy for Brooke to forget the rumors about his personal life. And then, when Miranda suddenly broke up with him at the beginning of July, it was Brooke he turned to for support. Miranda ran a water-ski school and had fallen for another instructor, and Derek was devastated, the extent of which he revealed to Brooke only—although he also kept his sense of humor about the whole thing. He said, "Maybe the problem was that I don't have a boat."

It had been a pivotal moment in the evolution of their friendship, Brooke supposed, her first real glimpse of his vulnerability. And afterwards, she'd wonder if they would have developed a friendship at all were its foundation not built upon a few weeks of the illusion that Derek had the personal life of someone who wasn't a frat boy. Would she have felt as comfortable alone in his office late at night, after everyone else had left for the day? That evening he had her going over a speech that had been written for him, because, he said, Brooke had a way with words. Confessing, when she'd noted that he seemed unusually nervous about this routine address—he gave speeches all the time—about his breakup the night before.

"And it was on Skype," he said. "I know. That's bad enough, but then the screen froze and there she was with her face in this bizarre contortion, because she'd been in the middle of a sentence about how this water-ski guy could give her all the things I never could, and I honestly thought she was joking, because that was ridiculous, and why was her face like that? And then the connection came back and she didn't even know I'd missed what she'd said. She kept saying, 'So we're good now?' But how can we be good after she broke up with me? I just don't understand it."

He'd been blindsided, he said, left wondering if he had any instincts at all, and his confidence was thrown. He wasn't sure he was capable now of getting up in front of hundreds of people and giving a speech, so he made Brooke watch while he practiced faking it, over and over. It really was the first time she had been there for him as a human being, a friend, rather than just an employee.

"You're doing great," she told him, after he'd run through the presentation for the fifth time, and he still didn't believe her, convinced that everyone could see right through him, even though he sounded just as assured and convincing as he ever did.

She would talk about the experience afterwards with Anjali, not sharing every detail, because some of it was personal. This was a continuation of a conversation the girls had been having all summer as they tried to figure out who Derek Murdoch was, what made him tick.

"I think he really just needs someone he can lean on," she said to Anjali. "Everybody leans on him, but who's he got to turn to?"

"Oh, but I'd say he's doing okay," Anjali answered. "Because he's been turning to Kelly and Eliza all summer long." Then she made a panicked face and said, "Don't tell them I told you. No one is supposed to know. They don't even know about each other, but they told me, and I can't believe I've kept my mouth shut until now."

They were out in the park, just the two of them, and Brooke didn't want to believe it. It was impossible—lies and gossip—because wouldn't she have realized that something was going on? Plus he'd never tried anything with her. But then she began to consider all the reasons it might not be impossible—the awkward moments among the group that summer, strange silences, weird behavior, and rumors from years before—and then there was the truth staring her right in the face.

By mid-August, Eliza had quit the internship (or maybe she'd been asked to leave, no one would say), and now Kelly didn't come for lunch in the park anymore. Nobody else seemed particularly bothered by what had transpired, so Brooke tried to play along, act like it was no big deal, even though she felt like an idiot, and had a hard time acting natural around Derek. It was like she was the one who'd been betrayed, even if it was just that she had these old-fashioned ideas about relationships and monogamy, without any real experience of either.

Derek could tell that something was up, though, and he wanted to know. She mattered that much to him. He called her into his office to find out what was going on, why she had been giving him the cold shoulder.

She said, "It's nothing." It would feel dumb and childish to admit how much Derek had disappointed her, and she had learned a lesson from the whole experience, which was to not infer promises that nobody had ever made to her.

He said, "Something's wrong. I can see it." He asked her, "Is this about the drama with Kelly?"

She cracked. "The whole thing makes me feel like such a fool." All that time she'd spent sitting in this very chair trying to soothe his heartbreak about Miranda, and he'd been getting it on with her colleagues.

He said, "But none of that has anything to do with you. And yeah, I've been careless—it's a fact. It's been a tough summer, and you know that better than anyone. I'm not proud of myself, but this doesn't change things, especially between you and me. Surely you know that." *You and me,* he'd said, magic words that made the drama with Kelly feel like something that could be easily tossed aside.

And even his carelessness Brooke could construe as noble. Because of course, with all the focus on the big picture and pressing issues, the rest of his life had been neglected and was kind of a mess. His mother still bought his clothes, delivering shirts to the office in big shopping bags on her trips to the city. Unless someone delivered lunch to his desk, Derek never thought about eating. The parameters of his job meant that he just didn't have the bandwidth to focus on those details, things like clothes, or meals, or being part of a meaningful relationship.

Plus, he was charming—smart and funny, just self-deprecating enough to put everyone at ease—so it was understandable that women responded as they did, and it wasn't as though Kelly and Eliza hadn't known what they were getting into. What had happened was all just part of the vibe, the charged atmosphere, late nights, the drinking. The rules were different in the political sphere. It was just the way things were.

But not everybody agreed. "He's thirty-five years old," said Anjali.

"He doesn't act it," said Brooke.

Anjali said, "Well, that's the problem."

Except Brooke wasn't sure. From where she stood, acting like a thirty-five-year-old seemed overrated. It required shutting down possibilities, committing to the status quo, and going to bed early. To get older but not grow old seemed like the best of both worlds, and she wanted to be like that.

"You're never going to be like that," said Anjali. "You'd never get away with it, because you're a woman."

By this point, Brooke was firmly on Team Derek. Sure, he liked to have fun, and his choices weren't always responsible. It might be all right for a college student to drink too much and end up on the dance floor at Slappin' Nellie's with some girl who wasn't wearing much more than underwear, but it wasn't exactly distinguished behavior for an elected official in his mid-thirties, particularly when the girl was almost half his age.

But—as everybody always said when the potential problem of Derek's partying was broached, because it often was—at the end of the day, he needed an outlet. And is it fair to hold it against a person that he just happens to be an unmarried heterosexual male? It's not like the crowd at Slappin' Nellie's was the type to turn their noses up at his behavior. Sometimes someone would show up with a camera, or a member of the press would try to get in for an exposé, but Derek's best friend Brent was always able to put a stop to that. A big guy who towered over Derek and everybody else, Brent had been watching out for him for years, since elementary school, when other kids had made fun of Derek's scars and taunted him with the nickname "Fire Boy."

So in terms of PR, they got off lucky in Derek's office. Many of his older colleagues in government had worse records of sexual impropriety and entitlement, and their staff had the extra trick of having to keep it all from their wives. With Derek, it was different—everybody liked him, it was all consensual. There were rumors about his reputation, but nothing substantiated, and none of it unethical or illegal—he wasn't a liar, he wasn't a cheater. He was also open about his personal life, and would end up confessing over beers, when it was just him and Brooke, that he was tired of it all.

"Plus, you're making me feel guilty," he said. "There it is. Right there. That look. Like you're judging." He'd got together with a volunteer the weekend before at the party convention. The summer was over by then, and Brooke was back at school, but she was still working in the office part time, and she'd been at the convention too. The volunteer had been a vapid idiot, the kind who wasn't interested in politics at all beyond the opportunity to prey on guys like Derek. The kind of girl who would lower herself to saying anything just to get a bit closer to power.

"I'm not judging," said Brooke, and she wasn't. Or at least she wasn't judging *Derek*, because she understood now. He could be careless. He needed outlets. "Besides, why does it matter what I think anyway?"

"Of course it matters," he said. "But I was just having a little fun. It always seems like such a good idea at the time."

"As long as you're both on the same page," she said.

He said, "See, that's what I love about you—you get it. Honestly, what would I do without you, Brooke?" With his puppy eyes, and those scars that had never managed to completely fade, he'd make her feel like she'd won a prize or something, in being the one who could help him hurt a little less. Derek gave so much to everyone that giving this one thing back to him—her understanding—seemed like the least that she could do.

"Why is everyone who works in this office a woman, though?" people would ask, people who'd heard the rumors and didn't like what Derek was all about. (And what Derek was all about, by the way, was equality, eradication of poverty, giving a voice to marginalized people, and giving everyone the tools to lift themselves up—and those people usually didn't like that, either.)

Brooke would have to emphasize the importance of giving women opportunities to enter politics, an arena from which they'd traditionally been excluded. It was an old boy's club, yes, pretty much everywhere, but not in Derek Murdoch's office—and who would have the nerve to criticize that?

"Okay then, why are all the women under twenty-five?" A valid question, but one that ignored the realities of politics, where pretty much everybody was under twenty-five, because everyone older than that was burnt out and could no longer afford to live on the paltry salaries. Derek surrounded himself with women because he respected and valued them, and not because he didn't.

Brooke would end up working for Derek for four years, as a part-timer during school breaks, and then full time after she graduated, and while he certainly had his flaws, he was always good to her; the closer their friendship became, the clearer it was he was one of the most honorable people she knew. Always striving to be a better man—he'd been trying to cut down on his drinking, because another election was on the horizon, and he had to be in peak physical form for that. He started running again in the mornings, and some days she'd join him because her place wasn't too far from his condo, and she only liked to run with company. But that didn't last long, because it was hard to keep up with Derek. Brooke didn't have his drive—nobody did. Which must have made it lonely out there, she thought, so many mornings where there was nobody but him.

She had a boyfriend at the time, which made things simpler. He also worked for the party, and it's true that Brooke's universe had become a bubble—everything was about politics, and even at school she'd joined the campus political clubs, losing touch with the friends she'd met in residence in her first year because they just didn't get it, how politics was like a game you had to always be playing. "There's more to life," she was repeatedly reminded by those friends, but these were people who didn't know how politics really *is* life—life-or-death in some circumstances—and how, as part of Derek's team, she was doing things that really mattered, so far beyond the stakes of, say, taking up knitting or badminton. Why would anyone opt to sit on the sidelines?

They were all in it together, and that's why it didn't matter that Derek mainly hired women to work in the office, or that he was older than she was. Lots of people were older than she was, and for the first time Brooke was being taken seriously, and it was *because* of her youth and perspective. Derek was interested in what she had to say and, unlike most people who were older, he wasn't afraid to shift his opinions, to learn from other people, to change his mind. "It's called being progressive," he used to say, "but what a lot of people forget is that 'progress' is supposed to be a verb. You've got to demonstrate it."

But it was always going to happen, Derek and Brooke. He even said that once, that he'd known it right down the line, and she'd felt it too. And, strangely, the longer it didn't happen, the more certain it seemed that eventually it would. She'd never met anybody who looked at her the way he did, who made her feel like the kind of person she'd always wanted to be. Even knowing everything she would come to know, she probably would have stood in line for a chance to be with him. And in certain framings of the situation, she supposed, this is exactly what she did.

Wednesday Afternoon

She had the late shift that day at the library, so she didn't have to hurry out of bed in the morning, and the newspapers were already strung up and on display when she came in to work at noon. *MURDOCH ALLEGATIONS ROCK PARTY*, headlines screamed, still in all-caps. Below was a photo of Slappin' Nellie's in poor light, dark and sordid. *Small-town bar where the hookups happened,* said the caption.

Lindsay came up behind Brooke. "That whole place is a trash heap," she said. "You see the girls lined up outside, crop tops in the freezing cold. They're all trying so hard. It's depressing."

Brooke glanced at her, but said nothing, and then Lindsay reached around to pick up the paper and open its pages. There was Derek on page A2, looking assured and confident, back when he was on top of the world. "I used to know him," she said. "Or kind of. I'd just gone into high school, but one of my friends babysat his sisters. His brother too. I think his mom was away and he was in the hospital— I remember that. It was in all the newspapers. At Christmas, we all gave donations to the charity fund."

"He got better," said Brooke.

Lindsay said, "He did." And Brooke was irritated that Lindsay figured she knew Derek better than Brooke did because her friend had babysat his sisters thirty years ago. "They're saying he'll be resigning today."

"They?" Could he really do it? Would he? It would upend the world, if this happened—or at least Brooke's sense of it.

Lindsay said, "It's everywhere online. He should have done it the other night though. I don't know what he thought was going to happen."

"He was trying to clear his name," said Brooke.

"But there's no coming back after that. How could he? I mean, you see his face now, it's what you think of. I mean, that press conference was not the performance of an inno- cent man."

Brooke admitted, "I don't really know what happened there."

"Those are the photos I remember," said Lindsay, point- ing to the paper. From back when he was in the hospital, reprinted farther down the page.

Before Brooke's time. She reminded Lindsay, "But the fire was a long time ago." Lindsay didn't understand.

———

That afternoon, she sat at the circulation desk and did a swath of check-outs for moms and babies after Morgan's story time—board books, lullaby CDs, and tomes on how to make babies go to sleep, mostly. She'd never realized it was such a complicated subject, sleeping, but the library had a whole shelf and a half of books about it, patented techniques. She couldn't imagine how this was a thing, or how something as instinctual as sleeping could require hundreds of pages to get down pat. Olivia, the kid she babysat, was older, and usually fell asleep on the couch while they were watching TV, and Brooke would have to carry her upstairs to her bed. But then maybe it was just the demographic, women like the ones in Brooke's lineup who had all the time in the world and yet were still rushing to get home in time for their babies' naps—the kind of women who tended to overcomplicate everything.

"He's so tired," one of the mothers told Brooke as she checked out a copy of *Moo, Baa, La La La!*, pushing the stroller forward and backward to get her fussy baby to soothe. "But he can't fall asleep yet." She waved a toy centipede in his face, tiny legs flying and bells jingling, and the baby only fussed louder. "No, he can't!" she sang in a merry little voice, and Brooke wasn't sure why he couldn't. Did it really have to be this hard?

A long line of babies before her now, as on every Wednesday, fat and bald, weird-looking and adorable, with their stressed-out, disheveled mothers. "He's seven months today!" one of them told Brooke, baby balanced on her ample hip as she picked up a stack of books in the other,

and Brooke smiled at them both, feeling somehow connected and also worlds away.

Her phone buzzed in her pocket, a new Derek alert,
and she checked it once the line had cleared and the library
was quiet. He'd be holding a news conference, it said, but
maybe she'd already missed it. She searched online for the
livestream, which was easy to find because it was everyone's
top story. Derek looking even worse than the other night,
if that was possible, but maybe it was the point—not defi-
ance, but contrition. This was careful. This was calculated.
The other night was reckless, but he would not be caught
off guard again.

"For the sake of the party, and the work we're doing . . ."
Brooke couldn't hear him because this was the library and
so the sound was off, but the words were captioned below
him, a staccato flow. He was really going to do it.

"Because this has become a distraction, and it's become
about me, which is undermining the good work of a lot of
people, and I'm not going to let that happen. So that is the
reason I'm resigning today as leader of the party. I'm still
intent on saving my reputation and defending my name
from these heinous allegations, but I also believe the best
path forward is me clearing my name outside of the spotlight of leadership."

The news was a blow, and also dizzying—how to orient
herself in this new reality? And she could only imagine how
Derek must feel, after everything they'd worked toward.
She recalled the campaign and how winning the leadership had seemed inevitable, because how could you work

so hard for something and not succeed? It was like how she used to believe that society and the world would just keep getting better—that proverbial arc that bends toward justice. But here was a setback—it had all come to nothing.

"I owe this to my colleagues, and to the public, whom it has been an absolute honor and privilege to serve these last few years," Derek was saying. "And I will continue to serve my constituents, while doing my utmost to restore their faith and trust in me. I appreciate all the support so many of you have shown me so far. I will not let you down."

And then he just stood there, staring into the camera. Staring right into her, it felt like, and the moment hung on long and awkward, silent. He was going to wait them out this time. He wasn't going to run. Then cameras started flashing, and reporters started shoving their microphones in his direction. No doubt they were questions about the mass resignation, about his political future.

All that effort and energy, and to have it just fizzle out—what a waste, Brooke was thinking. A waste for him, for her, and for everybody.

Someone must have been coaching him. He stayed still and then finally he spoke into his own mic. "I'm not taking any questions now," he said. His expression was calm. He said, "I think it's time to shift the focus." He waited a little bit more. "I want to thank you all for coming today." And then he turned and walked out, no longer a man who was running scared. Nobody chased him. All in all, his performance had been good.

But still—he'd resigned the leadership. All those years—
it had been her life—but he'd thrown it away.

Morgan came up from her lunch. "He's resigned," she said.
"Did you see that?" And Brooke wasn't sure she would ever
get used to the contents of her heart being the stuff of current events and gossip.

She played dumb. She said, "Who?" and collapsed the
window on her screen.

"Your man," said Morgan. "The admirable Mister
Murdoch." Morgan was a punk-rock librarian with blue hair
and a ring through her lip, so it was hard to say where she
was going with this, where her politics lay. "Someone was
watching it without headphones downstairs. I had to tell
them to knock it off." The stacks were supposed to be silent.
"Did he ever try it with you?" Heavy brows raised above her
chunky glasses. She was going to wait for Brooke's answer—
Brooke had never seen Morgan be patient before. She said
nothing, and the eyebrows shot even higher. "He did!"

Brooke said, "He didn't."

"He was your boss, though," she said. "I saw your CV. I
hired you." She had—after Marijke, Derek's chief of staff,
put a call in to Municipal Affairs, and together they'd found
a job for Brooke, a soft place to land. Above and beyond
what was required of them, she knew it. And yet.

A patron arrived with a stack of Caribbean travel guides,
and Brooke checked them out for him. What a thing it
would be to just fly away.

"So you worked for him," Morgan said, once they were alone again. "You think there's any truth to it all?" This was becoming exhausting, even painful—to keep having to put into words that Derek Murdoch was indeed a man of impeccable character, absolutely the real thing, the most inspiring person she'd ever met in her life. Not that it wasn't true, but it was worse that it was. And also because every time she said it, everybody thought it was because she was twenty-three.

"The whole thing's a setup," she told Morgan.

Morgan looked surprised. "Believe Women," she reminded Brooke.

Brooke said, "But I'm a woman. What about believing me?"

Morgan paused. This was more complicated, Brooke knew, than anyone supposed, but then Morgan moved on, robbing the moment of its tension, getting to work taking a stack of folders off her desk, and bringing them over to the counter. "It's all over anyway," she said. "And he'll be fine. They always are. You just watch—his friends will be taking care of him."

But would they, really? From that disastrous press conference the other night, and the resignation of his staff, Brooke had the impression that Derek had become a pariah. A kind of kinship between them. Although for powerful men, it was true, supporters always came out of the woodwork, lucrative job offers and teaching gigs. No doubt he could always settle down and become a consultant. Men of far lesser character have transformed such stories into book deals.

But she didn't think that Derek would be after such a fate. She said, "I think it's different when you know someone." Trying to explain, because she didn't want Morgan to think she was a person who wouldn't normally side with women. This was new to her, this position, and it fit her awkwardly, because she was feminist, but so was Derek.

Morgan let her leave it at that, but then they'd all been handling Brooke carefully since she'd started at the library. Her colleagues were still confused, she knew, about why she was here, where she had come from. Parachuted in from the city, and she hadn't even gone to library school, but she had applicable experience—plus she'd taken a pay cut to get here, and she was good at the job, so it's not like she had cheated anyone. But it must have seemed strange when her CV was placed on the top of the pile and accorded special attention from the powers that be. There might have been other people Morgan had in mind for the job, but none of them was Brooke, and now here she was. She'd been hoping to build relationships moving forward, that her colleagues might be people who could become her friends, because heaven knows she needed some, but they were all still waiting for her to fill in the blanks, and Brooke wasn't ready to do that.

Morgan looked over Brooke's shoulder at the monitor, and reached around to maximize the window Brooke had been looking at before—stopped it in a moment where Derek was caught mid-expression, not the greatest look.

Morgan said, "I never understood how anyone could find him attractive."

Brooke closed the window altogether and *poof*, he disappeared.

She could have run away. She could have gone traveling, signed up for some international development program and scuttled off to South America to save the world like Carly, and people would have admired her. She could have been posting shots on social media right now, selfies in bikinis on golden beaches, preserving sea turtle habitats or something. She might have begun to properly move forward with her life, except at this moment she knew she couldn't have stomached adventure—she was still far too broken for that.

A different kind of job would have kept her mind off things, though, something with fewer newspaper headlines and hours that weren't so open and empty. The library had rushes every so often, but it was either a mad crowd or the place was dead, save for a patron or two, and most of those patrons wanted very little to do with her, favoring the long-time staff members who already knew everybody's names. So there was all this time and space to think in, and what she would have given right now for any distraction. For the lineup at the check-out desk to stretch on forever, and she'd have to focus on the bar codes, taking care not to miss the thinnest volumes, minding the precarious stacks as she scanned one after another, ensuring none would topple over. Imagine a job like engineering. Imagine something as important as building a bridge.

She closed up with Morgan that night, flashing the lights for five, ten and fifteen-minute warnings—after that, they'd have to be more obvious, shaking the shoulder of a sleeping patron: "Wake up! The library is closed." People were often trying to hide in there, feet up on the toilet of the last stall in the bathroom, or skulking around the stacks in the hopes of not being caught. But then they'd send in Peter, the security guard at City Hall who Brooke had gone to high school with. He'd come over from across the street and do a final sweep, and then it was time to lock up and go home.

That night, Morgan was heading off in her own direction, and Peter stopped on the steps before returning to his post and asked Brooke, "You saw the news today?" And she would keep on taking these questions personally, even though the person asking just thought she was the proverbial woman on the street. He was everyone's boy, Derek, it was true. Brooke wasn't the only one in town who was feeling a sense of loss that day.

He said, "It's a shame. You think it's true?"

Brooke said, "Does it matter if it isn't?"

Peter asked, "You know, would you want to go out sometime?" He immediately backtracked. "I mean, nothing, like. . . . It doesn't have to be a big deal. I just thought. With you back in town. You know?"

She almost laughed. It was so preposterous. Not the fact of her going out with Peter himself, though it was that, too, but that he'd think she'd have the headspace for anything like that, the mechanical details of an ordinary life. She said, "Maybe sometime. Honestly, thank you. That's nice." It was. A reminder of how it might feel to be normal again.

But he knew she'd shut him down. Peter shuffled his feet, his big black boots. His uniform was designed to look official, but like his job, really, it was a knockoff. "See you tomorrow, Peter," she told him, and she began her walk across town toward home.

There was no food in her fridge, and while her dad would have been thrilled if she'd had dinner at Jake's two nights in a row, she wanted her parents not to be worrying about her for once. She stopped off at a corner store and bought a box of macaroni and cheese, a stick of butter, and a couple of Granny Smith apples, just to round out the meal. The apartment was dark, and she turned on all the lights so everything would seem less lonely. Lauren's shift wasn't finished until eight, and then she'd probably be going out with friends after. Perhaps Brooke should have taken Peter up on his offer after all. She wondered what that would have been like. Would he have worn his boots? And where would he have taken her—to Slappin' Nellie's? There was not a single establishment in this town that wasn't crowded with ghosts.

She made the macaroni and cheese and cut the apple into slices, and even sat down at the table to have her meal, rather than eating in front of the TV. She checked her messages—another one from Shondra Decker. Brooke had looked her up—she was legit; a reporter, like she said. And Brooke wondered where a reporter had gotten her email from, but didn't let wondering get in the way of finishing a bottle of wine, so that when she finally heard Lauren's key in the lock, she called out in a slurry voice that sounded strange even to her own ears.

"You're drunk," Lauren said. Brooke couldn't deny it. "Mind if I join you?" She got her own glass, unscrewed the cap from another bottle. Brooke had been scrolling through news and feeds on her phone all evening, waiting for a text from Derek that would never arrive. And this wasn't as sad as it sounded; it was more a comfort, familiar. Because Brooke was accustomed to waiting for Derek. She'd been doing it for years. It felt enough like home to begin to fill the void inside her—honestly, missing Derek was better than feeling nothing. The closest thing to love. Or maybe she just was drunk and maudlin.

Lauren must have seen it on her face—more perceptive than Brooke gave her credit for. She asked, "Who is it? Is he back in the city?" Brooke didn't know how to respond. Lauren said, "Is he a she?" Brooke shook her head. Lauren said, "I don't like to assume."

Lauren filled her glass and topped up Brooke's. She said, "I've been wondering what your story was. Knew there was something. I didn't want to pry. Was it a breakup?"

Brooke said, "Kind of." Wishing it was a straightforward situation that could be framed in those terms.

Lauren said, "Fuck it, right?"

Brooke said, "Exactly," and they clinked their glasses.

"DEREK MURDOCH IS MARRIED TO HIS JOB"

HOW IS IT POSSIBLE that the city's most eligible bachelor hasn't had a date in months? Although Derek Murdoch insists it hasn't been that long. He thinks some more, and asks, "What month is it, anyway?" And it's no surprise he's having trouble keeping track, because the weeks since his leadership victory have been a whirlwind. "There have been plenty of late nights at the office," he admits. "Right now, I'm focused on the job."

Murdoch's singular focus has always been key to his success. His trajectory in politics began before he was even eligible to vote. He was a political organizer and leader of a social justice youth group in his hometown of Lanark.

"For me," he says, "politics was never about the power. It's about what power gives you opportunities to do. It's actions that count—they're everything."

However, everything leaves little time for the rest of life, as Kim Nicholls, a former classmate, will attest. She was Derek Murdoch's high school prom date, and they were a couple during the following summer. "He was a good guy," she says, "but his mind was always someplace else. I was never his number one priority, and so we broke up."

"I'm not the easiest person to be with," Murdoch admits. "It would take a special kind of girl . . ." His voice trails off.

There were other girlfriends, some significant relationships, none of them long-term. Megan Gerhardt, who dated

Murdoch for a few months in 2001, remembers, "Derek was just all over the place. He was like the Energizer Bunny, and it was hard to keep up." They didn't stay in touch, but she shares photos from when they were a couple, Murdoch's grin taking up most of the shot. "He was always campaigning for something," says Gerhardt. "I kept waiting for the point when he would start to take our relationship as seriously as he took the rest of his life. And it never happened."

While his friends were beginning to settle down, Murdoch was celebrating his first election win as a city councilor in Lanark. He'd recently finished law school, but practicing law was not in the cards—he says, "I wanted to be in a position to really effect change."

Murdoch is godfather to his best friend's three children, who call him Uncle Dare, and he's close to his nephews. "I love kids," he says. "I'd love kids of my own, for sure. But right now—it's kind of a cliché—I'm married to my job."

These days Murdoch arrives at events escorted by his mother, or one of his sisters. "So you can't say I don't have plenty of women in my life," he insists, explaining that they taught him everything he knows about neckties and haircuts, and decorating his house in the country just outside Lanark. "I get a lot of advice," he confides. "Too much advice."

Yet his single status brings with it a certain longing. "When my father was my age, he'd been married for years," Murdoch says. "By then, he had four kids. My parents didn't have any money when they started out, and

my mom says they spent the first few years of their marriage living on love—and discounted pork chops. But they
made it work, and I want to live up to their standards. So
it seems strange that I don't have those things yet—a wife,
a family. I know it disappoints them. Sometimes it disappoints me."

Murdoch is about ten years older than most of the clientele here in this downtown coffee shop, but with his
youthful grin he fits right in. On top of working hard, he
stays in shape by running regularly and training for mara-
thons. Last year he completed his first Ironman, and he
says he's hooked. "I'm kind of an intense guy," he says.
"It's good to have an outlet." So there's time to train for a
triathlon, but he's too busy for a date?

"I still date sometimes," he said. "I haven't given up on
that yet."

He makes a point of attending church, and explains
that he finds services grounding, but also difficult. "Growing up, going to church was all about family," he says. "It
was the thing we did every week, without fail, and shined
our shoes for, and the entire week revolved around it."
In his teens, Murdoch would end up leaving his family's
church as a rejection of the denomination's restrictive
social views.

"But I missed my family," he said. "I missed that ritual
of all of us together, and even now there's an empty place
where that should be. I don't usually feel bad about not
having a family until I'm that one guy alone in a pew. I
mean, there's a reason there's pews and not chairs, you

know? You're not supposed to be on your own. And when I think about what I want as a family, that's what I'm thinking about."

He smiles and his face lights up: "One day."

Thursday Morning

He'd been booked on a morning show, the one where the hosts ask all the hard-hitting questions and they have the highest ratings. No doubt every morning show in the city had been vying to have Derek on, but Brooke thought he'd made the right choice with this one. He wasn't going to be coddled, and here he was taking responsibility for what was happening—the very opposite of that shambolic press conference three days before. He'd already resigned, but everything would not be lost. It was simply a matter of showing up and being accountable, and making voters remember why they liked him in the first place. Because voters really did like him, Brooke knew, and it was time to seize that popularity and use it to their advantage.

But their advantage was not *her* advantage, because, as she reminded herself again, none of this had anything to do with her. She hadn't even known about the interview until she woke up after eleven, her head sore from all the wine the night before. It was her day off, thank goodness, but poor Lauren had to go in to work, slamming the front door shut behind her. Which is what had disturbed Brooke's uneasy slumber—otherwise, she might have slept all day.

And now she was awake, empty hours looming, and she hadn't wanted to check her phone, because checking your phone should never be the first thing you do in the morning. But in this room, empty as the day was, what else was there for her to do, except bench presses? Not even a spot of sunlight to watch as it moved across the floor. No, the one object of interest within these four white walls was her phone, right there within arm's reach. So enticing, irresistible—even if her only messages were from her mom, her sister again, and the very persistent Shondra Decker. And then another Derek alert about a live-TV appearance, so Brooke sat up in bed and watched the clip. It was proof that Derek was alive, if not altogether well, and still in the world.

He was wearing a V-neck sweater, and he looked tired, but also comfortable, which was important in this context. Being comfortable made him far more credible, like he had nothing to hide, as he denied the allegations made against him, underlining that they were baseless, anonymous. He was still angry—Brooke could see the emotion just beneath the surface. But he managed to keep it contained as he answered the questions put to him.

"But what about the rumors?" asked the host, who was never going to go easy, but she was a woman, which would play well if everything went according to plan. "The ones about your propensity for relationships with young girls."

"Not young girls," said Derek. "Never underage."

"But teenagers."

"There were people I met when they were teenagers," Derek said, "that I'd become involved with later. But some of them, I met when *I* was a teenager, I mean. I've had relationships with girls in their twenties. I've had relationships with girls in their thirties. I've had relationships with girls in their *forties*."

"*Girls* in their forties?" the host asked.

Derek corrected himself. "Women. And I mean, it's not like I'm a casanova. If I was, I'd probably have been married by now—at least once." The studio audience laughed. "But I'm a political nerd, I'm a workaholic. I've never been the guy with smooth moves, but I've always respected women. It's how I was raised. My sisters are my two best friends. And I would never do these things they're accusing me of doing. These anonymous allegations, they're just not me. And anyone who knows me will tell you that."

"There have been rumors, though," the host persisted. "People are saying that. Stories about nights out back home—this is not the first time they've been raised."

"But what's that all about?" asked Derek. "The rumors. I mean, this is me back in Lanark, with my friends. The same people I've been friends with for decades. What are they saying, you know? What are the people who actually know about it saying? We like to have a good time, I'm not going to deny that. I mean, we specifically worked to build a local culture where people would want to go and have a good time and get together, and there's nothing wrong with that."

"But that's not what these allegations are about."

"These allegations are about nothing," said Derek. "You ask anyone who was there. I've made a point of living my life, being a man of my word. You build currency with that, right? People have faith in me. They know who I am." He looked at the camera. "You know who I am."

BEFORE

Brooke had known Derek for four years before anything romantic transpired between them—except for this one time the summer before, during a party at his house up north, and that certainly hadn't been *romantic*. Everyone else was gone, or passed out, scattered somewhere, and they were in the basement where he had a mini-theater set up, a big screen and a row of leather seats with cup holders. A terrible movie was playing, the one where Ben Affleck saves the world, the volume turned up loud because Derek's favorite song was, unabashedly, "I Don't Want to Miss a Thing." She had been sitting on his lap, and now she was straddling him, his chair reclined, his hands on her breasts. And they never got further than that, because someone smashed into the sliding door in the kitchen upstairs, glass flying everywhere, and they heard the explosion. He had to go up there to investigate and clean up and she'd fallen asleep at some point. They didn't talk about it in the morning, or ever after.

She wasn't sure if he even remembered it had happened. Once they were back at work they went on as usual—so maybe it really had been nothing. This was all during what would end up being the most intense year of her life, the year she spent working on Derek's leadership campaign. She'd finished school and was hired on full time, and during all those years she'd been working for Derek, she'd been watching him grow up too, albeit belatedly, and it was about time. But she'd been there and seen it happen. It meant something to her, the way he'd been handed responsibility and decided to live up to it. He was drinking less, trying to balance his work life with healthy habits. The atmosphere in his office was less like a party than it had been once upon a time, and even though Derek hadn't yet made the big life changes so many of his colleagues and contemporaries had—things like marriage, and parenthood—he seemed to have become more subdued. Now he was known to say things like, "I guess I'll call it a night," and he no longer stumbled into work in the morning hungover.

"The truth, though," he confided to Brooke one evening when it was just the two of them out for a drink and he'd ordered a Coke, "is that I just can't do it anymore. I'm getting old, Brooke. I used to bounce back like a rubber ball, but these days it just sucks the life out of me." He was depressed anyway, because his doctor suspected he had irritable bowel syndrome. "And that's not exactly on-brand now, right?" He was smiling, he was joking—but not entirely.

Brooke sipped her whiskey sour and Derek looked at her intently. "I so envy you," he said, "having everything before you."

"Oh, come on," she said. "You're not exactly washed up." She wasn't about to go in for the flattery. She had known Derek too long, and he was too important to her, which meant the things they talked about should only be real things. And she refused to be one of those girls.

"You can deny it all you want," he said. "Or at least I've tried to. 'Age is just a number' and all that, which was the kind of thing I really believed when I was trying to do things—to prove myself—when I was in my teens, in my twenties. But there comes this point when believing it doesn't even matter, because the body knows. You can't stave it off, and there you are: you're old."

"Derek, give me a break," she told him, signaling to the waitress to bring her another drink. "You're a guy," she reminded him. "Or maybe you've forgotten. Perhaps you're confused and believe it's you who has been made the target for 'age-defying' skincare products and Hollywood movies with the subtext that women are washed up at thirty-six and can only be cast as suburban mothers driving minivans."

"But it's the same thing," he said.

"No, it's not," said Brooke. "Male actors get to be leading men when they're in their seventies. Men get wrinkles and gray hair and they get to be distinguished. You get old, Derek, and people see you as experienced. It compounds your authority." Brooke had taken a course on gender and aging in third year. "It's only a matter of time before I audition for a movie and get cast as somebody's spinster aunt."

"You're twenty-two," he said.

"But my love interest would be a guy who's nearly forty. And somehow it balances out that way."

"Doesn't sound unreasonable," Derek said.

"Well, it wouldn't," she told him. "Not to you. Maybe you watch too many movies."

"So it wouldn't be so implausible, then."

"What?"

"You and me." There had been insinuations before, but never so direct, and not when he was sober. She had tried never to take them seriously, and blowing off comments like this was a reflex, though it had been easier just to humor him when he'd been sleeping with her colleague two desks over. She didn't want anything to happen between them until she was sure that it was real.

But Derek wasn't sleeping with anyone right now, as far as she knew, and he hadn't had a drink all night. The vibe was different, but she tried to fight it anyway. "Just because it's in a movie doesn't mean it's plausible. We've all seen movies, Derek."

"But I'm not talking about movies." His glass was empty, but he sipped his straw anyway for want of occupation. Brooke realized that, in this moment, he'd lost his swagger. No one got to see Derek like this very often, and certainly never when he was sober.

"Let's not do this," she said to him. The thing about Derek was that you had to remind him of the boundaries, because it was in his character to want to defy them, all of them, like a series of hurdles he was just compelled to leap.

"Do what?" Looking right at her with big eyes, and maybe it was the light in the bar or the way he held his head, but there was nothing strong or distinguished about Derek now. He could have passed for sixteen with that look, such naïveté. As if he really didn't know the answer to the question he was asking her. But always, always, Derek was smarter than he appeared.

"It doesn't work on me," she said. "The thing you do." It wasn't that she was immune to his charms, but that after all their years together, she understood the context better than most people.

"This isn't 'a thing I do,'" he said.

"Isn't it?"

"Sit here with my friend, who might just be the person who knows me better than anyone, and confess my most terrifying and vulnerable feelings and open myself up to the possibility of rejection? No, not exactly routine."

Brooke said, "Well, maybe that part is true. I don't think you've ever known the possibility of rejection in your life."

Derek said, "All the time."

"What?"

"Just because a person is determined to succeed doesn't mean he's not aware of the risks he's taking. I don't look down, Brooke, but I know what's there."

"What's there?" His eyes were locked on hers.

He said, "There is nothing. A terrifying abyss that could swallow you up, a great black hole. Everything I've worked for, everything I've ever wanted—gone. But I step forward anyway. You just do it. You can't think about odds."

"The odds of what?"

"That maybe there could possibly be something between you and me? Something real? And that maybe it could be the first real thing I've ever known in my whole life." It was hard to believe this was real, that it wasn't a joke. Was it a joke? "And I know," he said. "I know I'm messing with things here, taking a risk with our friendship, with work, and everything. And between us, it's never going to be easy, or straightforward. I don't even—" He stumbled on his words. "Um, I don't even really know what I'm trying to say here. What I'm doing." He was nervous. "I just—well, you know this would never be a traditional kind of relationship. But, I mean, if there is any possibility that you might feel the same way too—that this thing between us is something worth pursuing—I've got to know about it, you know? Because if I'm right—and I'm usually right, you know I am." He clasped his hands like a prayer. "Well, then, I can't miss this. To let you get away would be the stupidest thing I've ever done."

"But I'm not going anywhere," she said. And he took this as a promise, even though she meant it in practical terms, that he had no reason to fear he'd wake up tomorrow morning and she'd be gone. She also meant that they didn't need to rush this, make it into a production . . . but now he'd taken her hand, and she knew that this was going to be a production for sure, and all her resolve was crumbling in the face of this moment, which she had been thinking about for years.

As though she had written the script, to be honest. In invisible ink, maybe, and only in her mind. She'd never mentioned it to anybody (or even properly to herself), calling out anyone who'd dared to suggest it. But now they were there at the table and he was confessing his feelings for her, and it was almost familiar. And not because Derek fell for girls the way trees fell in the forest, because this felt different, sober and stressful. And Brooke had all the power here, to make or break whatever was blossoming between them. He was waiting to hear what she had to say.

"I'm not going anywhere," she said again, and what she meant this time was *I'm yours*.

He was holding her hand, and he said, "What do we do now?"

She said, "I don't know."

"I need a drink," he said.

"Might be a good idea." She ordered another one too, and they were quiet when the drinks arrived. Which was strange, because they were never quiet together. They were always arguing about something, talking, discussing, but nothing was pressing now. Everything important had already been said. Derek took her hand again, and didn't let it go, even when the tables filled up all around them and anybody could have seen.

It had been her. All along, right down the line. It felt like a song, or a movie after all, kind of cheesy, which had never been her kind of narrative. The people she'd hooked up with before had never gone in for grand gestures, and there hadn't been any forethought to what happened between them. Most of the time she'd just woken up in the morning beside someone new and supposed, "Well, here goes nothing." Which usually turned out to be the case.

But this was different, which was why she and Derek didn't know what to do with themselves, and even once the drinks were gone and their nerves were less taut, she still didn't know how to be.

"What's up with that?" she asked Derek, about their awkwardness. He'd paid the bill and they were walking out of there, his hand on her back. "I thought you had moves for every situation."

"This is kind of a new situation," he said. He was years older than she was, but he seemed like a little boy, and it felt like she was the one with the experience here, but she wasn't. Still, she knew what to do.

"You could kiss me," she said. "It would be a good start." Which made her sound more cool and assured than she really was, because her legs were shaking so stupidly with nerves she was practically tap dancing. And there she and Derek were, out on the sidewalk for anyone to see, except the street was empty. It was late, and they were the only two in the world.

And a kiss—Derek knew how to do this. Closing his eyes, and bringing his face toward hers, that face she'd seen a thousand times. It was like coming home, and she kept her eyes open, and they kissed so much that by the time they stopped it seemed like they had traveled a long way.

———

And that was it, for a while at least. He walked her back to her house and kissed her again, goodbye at the door, which felt right. His behavior had been gentlemanly, she would remind her best friend Carly days later, when Carly warned her about the trouble she was getting into. But that first night, Brooke didn't want to tell anybody yet. She went upstairs and got ready for bed, her mind a bit spinny, not from drinks, but exhilaration. Butterflies in her stomach as she replayed the evening in her mind.

What did it mean that he'd left it at just a kiss at the door? And in the days that followed, when everything between them remained up in the air, she regretted that she hadn't pressed the point, that she hadn't brought him upstairs with her, just to establish whether this was one thing or the other. So that at least she'd have it to hold on to, a memory of one tangible thing, even if this turned out to be another situation where they never talked about it again, like the last time. But it didn't feel like that—or was this only wishful thinking? How could she be sure?

She couldn't get him alone. As days went by, there were stolen glances and his secret texts: *I can't stop thinking about kissing you.* His hand on her arm, nothing she ever would have noticed before, but now his touch was electric—how could everybody around them not feel it too? But nobody did, which was a relief, because she liked the idea of this, whatever it was, being just theirs.

Everyone in the office was distracted anyway, focused on other things. Derek was introducing a bill to make gun violence a public health issue, a controversial motion that would probably not pass, but the issue was important, and there was enough support for it on the other side that they had a chance of success. They were busy with lobbying, presentations, consultations, and research, and it was so all-consuming that there were moments where it slipped her mind—his words, his touch, that kiss—but only ever for a second or two, and she'd be back again, daydreaming. Had it really happened at all?

But it was real, as affirmed by those looks, the way her body responded to his hand on the small of her back as they'd enter a room together. And by his texts, especially the one she'd received from him the morning after the night he'd kissed her on the sidewalk—*I want to take this slow. And I don't want to mess this up. But last night was really important, and I can't wait to do it again.*

He wasn't avoiding her, he told her. Everything that was keeping them apart now was only circumstantial, and when they finally managed to be alone together, the two of them in his office with the door shut, both drunk on the tension between them, he explained just why he wanted them to take their time. She wanted to jump him, then and there, but he was the one holding back. "And it's weird for me, to not just want to bound ahead—you know that slow is not my speed. But with you, I just want to take in everything we have right now, for the sake of right now and not just to get to the next thing. It's just that there's no rush, I think."

And Brooke agreed—but also she didn't. She really did want to get to the next thing, and kept waiting for chance encounters, a secret tryst in the photocopier room when no one else was looking. But Derek was using the utmost discretion, refusing to be tempted by her tight sweater and her pencil skirt, and he was adamant that none of this would be cheap and tawdry. They had to get through the week, he said, until the bill was read, and then he'd be able to turn his attention to this fully. "Tomorrow night," he promised, a week after his confession and their kiss. He'd stopped by her desk, when no one was around, and said that finally he was ready to confront this. "I'd love to take you out for dinner." She had plans with friends, but those could be canceled. She'd already blown them off the week before because of work things, so they practically expected it now.

She said, "Sounds good," and tried not to seem too eager, too needy. She'd always been the levelheaded one, and she didn't want to give that up, her single advantage.

He wanted to pick her up at her place, but it wouldn't have looked right, and her roommates would ask questions. So instead they met at a restaurant after work—he'd come straight from meetings. It was a place not far from the office, a café with super-attentive waitstaff and fuchsia wallpaper with a flamingo print. Derek had secured a booth with lots of privacy, and ordered oysters and a bottle of wine that cost a third of Brooke's rent. "It's a special occasion," he told her. "Finally."

"It's been quite a week," she said.

"Oh, I know it," he said. "Everything. Work, and the bill. Us."

"Us."

"So I've decided," he said, "that instead of just being an idiot who doesn't know what he's doing, I'm going to pretend that I do."

"You're not really convincing me," said Brooke.

"I've been thinking about it all week," he said. "Everything. Kissing you. And thinking about where we go from here." He would be as methodical about this as he was about everything that mattered to him.

Which meant that she'd have to take over managing this project or they'd never get anywhere, because romance wasn't policy. She said, "Well, I have some ideas."

They didn't even finish the wine, skipped dessert—the oysters were filling enough. They were in a hurry to get where they were going, which was back to Derek's condo, where she'd been many times before.

They'd been kissing in the cab, in the elevator, against the wall in the hallway, and now here they were. His hands were under her shirt. He said, "I've thought about this so many times."

"This week."

He said, "This week, and always. I don't remember when I didn't—" He pulled away from her and looked at her. "You're amazing, you know that? I've always thought that. And now you're here."

But they had been together like this before, that other time, in his basement in the summer.

He said, "I was clueless then. I'm sorry. I knew we needed to get here, but I didn't know the way. Plus, there was Trevor." Brooke's boyfriend, who'd worked in their office as a data analyst, but he'd left and moved to China to teach English to kindergarteners, so there was a Trevor no longer, and neither she nor Derek was drunk, or at least they hadn't been when they'd started this evening, and some of that wine had been left in the bottle. Sitting on the edge of his bed, they were both clearheaded, which was important, but it made things difficult too. She lay her phone down on the bedside table, and imagined it could belong there. Then she started unbuttoning his shirt.

He said, "Slow. I mean." The ridges on his chest, an unknown topography.

She was nervous about it too, because she didn't know what to expect.

And now his comment had alarmed her. "Does it hurt?" she asked. The scars. She didn't know. He'd pushed her hands away.

He said, "No. I just." He moved to turn the light out, but she held him back.

"But I want to see," she said.

He said, "You really don't." Grimacing as she unfastened the rest of his buttons, which certainly dampened the mood, but she didn't stop, because she didn't want him to think he had anything to hide. The way he always did, about his scars, which was so unlike him because he was open about everything else, the stories he told about the pain that didn't show, and how it powered the work that he did. But the scars from the fire were different. He had a giant hot tub at his place up north, but he never went in it. He'd dated a woman who ran a water-ski school, but Derek wouldn't even jump in the lake.

"It's awful," he said to her now.

"It's not," Brooke promised him. It wasn't. She'd shaken off her own shirt, and he unfastened her bra, and she put her arms around him, their skin pressed together. She moved down to kiss his shoulders, his chest, and then she felt his body seize, like this was torture. She returned to his face then, his lips, this kissing. Running her hands down his back, his skin like no other skin she'd felt before. Pink and scarred, those ridges, still looking raw, although it had been that way for so many years. The skin he had. A body's ability to repair itself comes with limits, and Derek knew these, even after years of painful surgeries. And Brooke thought about that boy in the hospital, how young and unformed he'd been, and the ways in which the accident had made him. An unscarred Derek Murdoch would have been somebody else altogether.

She said, "I love your skin. I love your scars. I love your body, all of it." They'd moved to his bed, and he was kissing her chest, her nipple in his mouth, and then the other.

He said, "Your body is incredible."

And she said, "I love you," by accident, and kept talking so instead the sentence she'd uttered was "I love your body." Again. Also true, and less embarrassing. Pulling off the rest of his clothes, and taking him in her mouth—the way he moaned. As though she hadn't known Derek Murdoch until this very moment of sheer vulnerability, and it was laid bare now. He was gorgeous, and sweet, and he touched her body with his characteristic care and consideration.

Derek in his life never did a single thing halfway, and so it was incredible and magical what happened between them, but her very favorite part was waking up beside him in the morning.

Thursday Afternoon

Recalling that feeling of closeness and satiety that first morning they spent together only underlined the hollowness of the moment now as Brooke sat alone in a basement watching Derek on TV, her whole life in pieces around her—and now his life was broken too. If she had known then what was in store for them, would she still have let any of it happen? Could she have dared to laugh him off that night at the bar with the Coke when he took her hand, and then gone—alone—on her merry way? A thing to entertain, this notion that any other destiny was possible, that she could have fought what was coming, but she knew it was ridiculous. Even now, after all that she'd learned, she was still invested in what was going to happen to them, and waiting for the twist before the end, the part where everything between them—this impossible dream—would somewhere turn out okay.

From the start, she had imagined that intimacy with Derek—finally moving past the image and persona to see his skin, to touch and taste it—would clarify things. She'd had this feeling that maybe sex would be the key to understanding him properly, Derek at his most essential, and finally she would be able to hold together all the other disparate impressions of him at once. But it only made things more difficult, because once she'd glimpsed this side of him that so few others got to see, it only compounded her sense that none of it was real.

He was an incredible performer—all the speeches, the rallies, the parties he'd hosted on evenings when he was thoroughly exhausted. The way he led them all in the party, in the office—authority was a performance too. And when they were together, just the two of them, late nights together in his bed after hours of working, and the pleasure and release he received from her body, from both of them together—it was so convincing . . . but then it all was. And Brooke wondered again what he thought about when he was alone, if Derek had much of an inner life at all, because she had rarely seen a glimpse of it.

On TV that morning he'd been more composed, as though he had some control of the narrative again, and she hoped this was true. She hoped that this interview would overwrite his performance at the press conference and that maybe all this really would blow over. *Girls in their forties*, though. That had been a slip. And wasn't true, as far as she could recall. Maybe he'd dated someone twenty years ago who was in her forties now?

Her phone rang—actually *rang*, an unfamiliar sound, as she barely knew her own ringtone—disturbing the silence and making her jump. An unknown number—who was calling her? It was a question she didn't even think to ask, because she knew. It would be him. *Finally.* Derek wasn't one for phone calls usually, even though he was old enough to be, but then he wasn't one for emotional performances on breakfast television either, so all things were possible. She'd just seen him on TV, as close as they'd been in weeks, and it made sense that he'd be thinking of her too.

But it was someone else, a woman's voice, not Nicole. "Is this Brooke Ellis?" she asked, and Brooke wanted to answer, "Who's asking?" but her first instinct, as always, was not to be rude.

"You're a hard one to track down," the woman said. "But I got your number from a friend of yours. Diamond? Found her in a local Facebook group." Goddamn Jacqui Whynacht.

"I won't take more than a minute of your time," the woman said. "My name is Shondra Decker, and I'm a reporter with the *Daily Observer*. I think you've been getting my emails?"

Brooke said, "What's this about?"

Shondra Decker said, "I wanted to talk to you about Derek Murdoch. I understand you worked for him."

"We worked together, yes."

"I wanted to ask you some questions, in the context of the allegations against him now. About the workplace

environment, if you had experiences of harassment, anything inappropriate. That kind of thing."

Brooke said, "I don't have anything to say to you." And
she should have just hung up there, but she hadn't been
brought up that way. At that moment, she was ruing her
mother's lessons.

Shondra Decker was saying, "Nothing? Because my
understanding is that the two of you had a particularly close
relationship." What kind of an understanding, exactly?
"And I just feel like you might have a unique perspective
on this story, a way to round the whole thing out. Add a bit
of, I don't know, some nuance."

"Nuance." Brooke shouldn't have answered the phone.
She didn't know where the woman was going with this, if it
was leading to the most obvious destination, the sorry
details of her personal life origamied into tabloid fodder.
Brooke had survived everything Derek had thrown at her
so far, but she did not want to have to face this. How could
he have abandoned her here?

The reporter said, "I would love to give you the opportunity to comment. Tell us your side of the story in your
own words. Your voice would really matter here." She was
right about that. Brooke knew things about Derek that
nobody else did, and this story was not as straightforward
as the press was presenting it. Perhaps the one benefit to
no longer being on the inside was that Brooke was finally
free to say what she wanted—and if she said it, maybe the
reporter would leave her alone.

But it would have to be simple. Brooke knew how a person's words could be twisted, and she didn't want to make things any worse than they already were. She told Shondra Decker, "Derek was never anything but a gentleman to me. He's one of the good guys. He's one of the best guys."

"But can you elaborate on your relationship?" the reporter asked.

Brooke said, "I have no further comment." She'd already said enough, more than enough. She had to cut the conversation off before she really got in trouble, so she ended the call, the reporter still in mid-sentence, even though Shondra's voice was the only one she'd heard all day that wasn't being broadcast from a television studio. And this sad state of affairs was why when her mother, who was possibly psychic, shortly afterwards sent a text commanding Brooke's appearance at home for lunch, she replied with *OK!* As short on excuses as on food in the fridge, and she had to escape that apartment, her loneliness, because there are only so many hours a person can spend underground observing passing feet. She too wanted to be part of the movement, the momentum. And now she had a destination, and there was something restorative about that, a reason to get dressed and brush her teeth, her hair. Locking the door behind her when she left, she rose to the overground. But of course, the world was very quiet, because it was a Thursday and the middle of the day. Everyone else had already arrived at where they needed to be.

The walk home was uphill, streets Brooke had known her whole life, and she avoided the direct route that would have taken her through downtown, past her father's restaurant and Slappin' Nellie's, where the vomit on the sidewalk from the night before was probably right now being rinsed off with a bucket of soapy water. She kept to the residential streets, some of them without even sidewalks, because extravehicular activities around here were always considered a bit suspect. If there were any neighbors home, they were probably all peering at her through their curtains now—but it seemed like everyone was out.

Her parents' house was quiet too, one car in the driveway and just an oil stain where her dad would park his car when he got home. Brooke climbed the steps to the door and hesitated for a moment, unsure of her jurisdiction. It had been this way since she'd moved back to town. Knocking didn't seem right, but just opening the door like this was her place and she lived here was too familiar when it felt so strange.

Luckily, she didn't have to decide either way, because the door flew open and her mother appeared. She had been looking for Brooke out the window. She was recently retired from her job at the high school, and the days were long for her now too. "What are you waiting for?" she asked, before enveloping her in a hug. "Brookie Cookie," she said, employing an old childhood nickname, and holding her daughter close far longer than was natural, underlining Brooke's certainty that her mother was worrying about her in a way that made Brooke feel guilty for the trouble. Her mother said, "I made soup."

Which is what she did, Brooke's mother, for all occasions, from head colds to Thanksgiving. She could conjure a soup out of anything, and today it was tomatoes and basil, the final harvest from her garden. She'd made grilled cheese sandwiches to go alongside, and they sat down together in the breakfast nook, which as a child Brooke had pretended was her office. When she was little, Brooke dreamed of growing up to be Melanie Griffith from *Working Girl*—which her mom still had on VHS—and now she didn't even have her own desk.

Her mother said, "Eat." And she didn't ask anything else so Brooke was able to eat, and the food was good, the cheese in the sandwiches so perfectly melted that it all held together. She needed to get around to learning how to cook, Brooke considered. When does that happen anyway? When do all these important life lessons begin to kick in?

Her mother said, "You watched it, then?" Of course she wanted to talk about the interview, the situation in general. And she wouldn't know what to say, exactly, or what she was really asking of Brooke. Brooke knew her mother had been waiting for months for her to explain what had happened at Derek's office, setting up all kinds of soup-adjacent opportunities for her to do so, but how could Brooke explain when even she didn't understand? Plus, it was embarrassing. What her mother really wanted was to be told that everything was okay, that her daughter was perfectly fine, and that Derek was the same honorable person they'd been supposing him to be. Both Brooke and her mother would have liked to go on believing that this was true, but maybe they'd finally reached a turning point. Her mother said, "I think it's over for him. I watched that interview, and it was all I could think about, those accusations."

"The accusations are ridiculous," Brooke reminded her.

Her mom said, "It doesn't matter. And you know what they say about smoke and fire."

"I don't know why they say it," Brooke told her. "It's not even a good metaphor. Where there's fire, there's smoke, it's true, but it's not always the case the other way around."

"I don't know if the metaphors are the problem," said her mom. She was sitting at the table with her hands together before her, leaning forward avidly. Her mother said, "How *are* you? And not just with Derek, and everything. I mean *you*." As though the two weren't impossibly intertwined. Symbiosis. Except symbiosis went both ways, and that wasn't always the case here. It was possible that entire days went by and Derek didn't think of her at all. "Your dad and I, we're worried about you," her mom continued.

"Not helpful," Brooke said. Pushing her plate away even though she wasn't finished eating. This conversation put her on guard.

"But we want to help," said her mom. "With you so close now, back home, we can. So why not? I don't know what you're trying to prove here."

"That I'm capable of taking care of myself?"

She said, "But you don't have to."

Brooke said, "I really do." They'd been through this before, but her mother never listened.

Her mother said, "I think it's for the best anyway."

"What?"

"That you got out of there when you did. Before it all fell apart. Imagine being there now, all those repercussions. He never did anything like that to you, right?"

"Mom, he never did anything like that to anybody."

"Because I wondered, I don't know. If that was the piece of the story we were missing."

"It's not a puzzle, Mom. It is what it is."

"It's just hard to understand," she said. "And you're not yourself—I can see that. I'm not stupid, Brooke."

Brooke said, "I'm just tired. We were up late, Lauren and me. Had some wine." She would give her mother this one morsel, because she knew she would savor it. Her mom would weave a cozy story out of it and imagine that here was the beginning of everything being okay.

Sure enough. "Lauren," said her mom. "So you're getting along, you two? Because I was worried about that too. I just don't know."

"You worry about everything."

"It's in my job description," said her mom. Right up there with making soup. "I'm glad you've got someone, though, to have fun with. You've got to have a social life."

"Oh, I do," said Brooke. "No, we're getting along great. She's . . . she's really great."

"Oh, great," her mother said. Too many greats. They were trying. Brooke's mom said, "You know Tina Skipton's selling her house, right? They're moving out west, or at least they're hoping to. And Heather Wilmington listed it. Derek's sister. She's married to Evelyne's friend's nephew." Lanark was a very small town. "Anyway, she's furious— Heather. She did an interview in the paper, and she said it's a political vendetta. She's a huge advertiser, with the real estate listings. I guess they had to print it. You think it's true, though? That they're out to get him?"

"Politics is nasty," Brooke told her. Derek would never admit it himself, or partake in the nastiness directly, but he was not above having other people do the dirty work for him. "It's a reality."

"Sounds like she's starting a campaign to support him, or a barbeque. I don't know."

"A barbeque for what?"

"You should read the article." She tilted her head toward the recycling box in the hallway where the *Weekly Adviser* had been flung atop a pyramid of meticulously rinsed jars and pop cans. Brooke's dad had a Diet Coke habit. "I don't know, he's her brother. If Nicole were in trouble, you would organize a barbeque."

"Nicole's a vegetarian."

"She wouldn't have to eat." What Brooke didn't say was that Nicole would never get in trouble. She was principal and proprietress of Little Feet Montessori School in a small town forty minutes west down the highway. She'd moved away, but she hadn't gone far, and she'd made a life that everybody understood and recognized, married to a guy adored by the whole family.

"Or a car wash." Her mom was kidding now. She was from the city, and moved to Lanark with her husband years ago, before Nicole and Brooke were born, and she had never stopped finding Lanark's small-town sensibility ridiculous. She only read the *Weekly Adviser* so she could make fun of it, reporting back on which of Brooke's felonious elementary school classmates had been written up in the court docket. "He's got the support, though. They wrote an editorial. This town loves him and he's worked hard to earn that currency. They're not about to give up just like that, no matter what happened ten years ago."

"Nothing happened."

"That's what I heard him say, before he ran away, all the way down those flights of stairs."

"It was not a good performance."

Brooke's mother said, "No." She said, "So we're on his side, our family? As official representatives of you?"

"There's no proof," said Brooke. "Just one woman's word."

"There's two," said my mother. "And I think it's interesting, the way a woman's word counts for nothing." She sounded disappointed. Maybe "interesting" wasn't the word for it.

"But it's not 'nothing,'" said Brooke, trying to explain. "It can't just be either/or—there is something in the middle. And they're being used, those women. No one cares about them, and they're going to be eviscerated, and now Derek's life is wrecked, like he's just some other guy. And it's personal for me. I know him. We were—we are—friends."

"How's he doing?" asked her mom.

Brooke picked up her sandwich again and ate what was left of it. Finally, she said, "I haven't really talked to him. A few texts. I think he's coming up for the weekend."

"And you're going to see him then?"

"I don't know." Her mother liked to push her into corners and watch her squirm. Aside from making soup and reading the *Weekly Adviser*, this study was her favorite pursuit.

That night Brooke was scheduled to babysit Olivia Tavares again, picking her up from her after-school program at 5:30, the sun already low on the horizon—the days were getting shorter. She was carrying Olivia's backpack because it was "too heavy," apparently, even though it was empty. Kids were funny, a distraction. They didn't care about politics, either, and while Brooke used to think that anyone who didn't care about politics was irresponsible at best, short on brain cells at worst, it turned out that these days they were her favorite people.

Walking home, Olivia didn't ominously ask Brooke how she was doing, or even how her day had gone, no small talk, chattering instead about the plastic charm necklaces that were all the rage these days, all the charms she longed for and hoped that her mother was going to buy her. Brooke didn't need to say a single word—it was almost like she wasn't there.

But when they got back to Olivia's house, unlocking the door with Marianna's spare key, boots in the vestibule, coats on the hooks, Brooke felt a visceral reaction to the living room. Because here was the scene of the crime, almost, three days that felt like a lifetime ago. She'd been sitting on the couch when her phone started going off, and she couldn't sit in that spot again because it was still too overwhelming. For the time being, she avoided the living room altogether.

She heated up leftover pasta for Olivia's dinner and then helped her with her math homework. She tidied the kitchen when everything was finished, while Olivia was having her allotted screen time before bed. Loading the dishwasher and wiping the counter, Brooke felt like she lived her whole life lately haunting other people's houses. She imagined what it would feel like if this life were hers, though, a life like Marianna's, working two jobs to support her daughter on her own. Olivia's dad had never been in the picture, taking off long ago when her mom was still pregnant.

"It's a funny thing," Marianna had once told Brooke. "If Olivia hadn't happened, I'm sure I wouldn't even remember him. He was barely a blip."

It would be exhausting, Brooke knew. She'd had the whole day to herself before coming over to babysit, and still she was tired once she'd put Olivia to bed. She came downstairs, to the living room, and collapsed on the easy chair—not on the couch. Her sister had texted and asked Brooke to call her, so she did, and they talked about their mother, about the anxiety Brooke had detected at her surface at lunch that afternoon, and they both, as they always did, considered the depths that lay beneath. Their mother's anxiety was how she showed her love, but this could also be a burden.

"Have you talked to him?" asked Nicole. She had also watched the clip from the morning show, Derek in a sweater, back to his old self. Or at least, that had been the intention.

And Brooke had to confess that no, she hadn't talked to him. She'd never been able to lie to Nicole, who would always see through her. The morning after she'd woken up beside Derek Murdoch for the very first time, Brooke had called her sister without even thinking about it, because there was no one she trusted better in the world.

And what Nicole had said was, "I don't know about this." Her voice tentative, but she was willing to be persuaded otherwise, to give Brooke and Derek the benefit of the doubt. But her first instinct was that this was going to end badly. "Of course, I trust your judgment," she'd told Brooke, "but it's the other guy I'm worried about." It was nothing about Derek personally, she insisted. Just that a person with so much on his plate could not give Brooke all that she deserved.

"But all I want is him," said Brooke.

"Okay," said Nicole, "but don't forget that you also deserve everything." Her own husband, Sean, was the nicest guy in the world. And yet—the one thing Brooke could not admit to her sister—Sean was also ordinary, and so was their life together, and Brooke wanted something different than all that for herself.

"Just don't get in over your head," Nicole had warned that first day, but it was too late for that, and all this time later, she was generous enough not to say "I told you so."

"DEREK MURDOCH: HE'S OUR MAN"

. . . AND WITH THIS LATEST SCANDAL, some are wondering if his luck has run out. Is the Golden Age of Derek Murdoch finally over?

Not yet. A look back at the progress and improvement Murdoch has delivered to Lanark over the past decade provides an unprecedented example of the kind of good a politician can do. Many lives in our community were made better, and to say that some were even saved is no overstatement. Murdoch has earned the right to have us stand by him during times of trial as we've supported him when it was so much to our advantage.

"We told you so," his detractors are telling us now, but imagine if we'd listened to them all along? How much poorer would this community be for such a failure of vision? So let's not fail ourselves, or Derek himself. He's been there for Lanark, and we resolve to return the favor when he needs it most.

Friday

Back before her life fell apart, Brooke used to have a digital calendar, the kind that divides every day into each quarter of an hour, and all of it was accounted for. She was a career girl, and she had meetings, and galas, and appointments, and field trips. She coordinated forums and panels and fact-gathering missions, and in those rare moments when she wasn't working, she scheduled appointments with herself to go to the gym. When making plans with friends, she could only book weeks in advance, but she wasn't even unusual in this respect. It was simply the pace of life in the city, and time was at a premium. A day was like a puzzle, the hours were its pieces, and at the end of every day she'd fall into bed exhausted, and she wasn't even among the busiest people she knew.

But everything was different now. She had all the days in the world, but none of the pieces, so the hours stretched long, and she felt very small inside them. Her mother had been urging her to keep busy, take classes, volunteer at the homeless shelter, and get back to being the daughter she recognized, but Brooke kept resisting. Partly because, yes, she probably was depressed—her mother wasn't wrong about that, but there was more to the story. Despite her mother's urging, Brooke didn't want to take her mind off things. There were certain things it was vital her mind be on, because she was still sorting it all out for herself, trying to make sense of what happened. And she supposed that all this sorting was the only way she knew to hold on to what she had lost. Beginning to move on with a new chapter of her life would be to acknowledge the rest of it was over, and she wasn't ready yet.

And so she did nothing, waking up to another morning in this apartment that wasn't hers, and she wondered what she was really waiting for. Checking her phone, she found an answer delivered in the form of a text from Derek. *Hey, you haven't heard from anybody, have you? I'll be back tonight. We need to connect.* A message that clarified nothing, because Brooke had no idea what he was talking about, not exactly. Was there even a door between them to open anymore? But she couldn't just ask him, because she didn't want him to think she was pushing too hard, which had been the problem between them even before everything else had gone so wrong. Instead, she had to continue to be cool. *Yes, and.* Engaging with Derek had always been more than a bit like high-school improv.

BEFORE

He'd been straightforward from the start, making sure that she knew what she was getting into with their arrangement. Brooke was aware that Derek wouldn't be able to give her many of the ordinary things that women expected from their partners—time, devotion, attention. Everything between them would be different, because of who he was and what he did, the relationship made even trickier because of her age, her job. "You know they look for any excuse for an attack," Derek reminded her as he explained why they would have to keep things under the radar, which sounded more reasonable to Brooke than it might have to most women, because politics was her business too.

And because keeping their relationship out of the public eye was hardly a sacrifice. It would be easier, really, to step away from the spotlight, all the scrutiny. Or at least this was how it had seemed at the start. Brooke knew where they stood, and she didn't need everyone else to know it too, didn't need to contend with the rumors and the whispers. Insinuations that this was part of a pattern, the same old thing—Derek with another girl, the latest office romance. They wouldn't understand, and nothing Brooke or Derek could say would convince people who were determined not to take their relationship seriously. Determined to believe this was just another fling. But Derek had promised it wasn't, and Brooke had known him for years by now. She would have been able to tell the difference. What they had was altogether new, and this was special, but also personal, and nobody's business but their own.

Brooke had enough trouble dealing with her friends anyway, who only claimed they were looking out for her best interests, but it didn't always seem like it. "Do you really want to go through life as someone's secret girlfriend?" asked Carly. She wasn't Derek's biggest fan, and the disconnect was mutual. She had worked for Derek during Brooke's second summer, which was how she and Brooke had met, but she only stayed for one season and ended up joining a nonprofit. Politics had left Carly disillusioned.

Brooke's housemates were more accepting than Carly, but then their house only had the one bathroom, so if she spent night after night at Derek's place, nobody minded, as long as she paid her share of the rent on time.

So she was alone in this, because even Derek brushed away her concerns about their relationship as things progressed, once it all started to seem more complicated than it had been solely in principle. She had been trying to

articulate her feelings and anxieties and make him understand how it was that she was feeling, perilously suspended,
but he didn't want to get into it. He would tell her to stop
overthinking everything. She was making it all too hard.

"You can answer this one question," he demanded of her.
"Is it working? And I'm not talking about next week, or six
months from now. I mean this moment." At that moment
they were drinking wine at the end of a long day at a healthcare conference in Boston, a view from the room overlook-
ing the harbor, room service just delivered, so of course it
was working. These rare and extraordinary occasions when
they got out of town were the closest they ever came to func-
tioning like a normal couple, even if it was awkward because
she had to book her own travel and wait for Derek to reim-
burse her from his personal account, because she obviously
couldn't afford it, and none of the people in the office were
supposed to know that he was paying because that wasn't
appropriate, but it was still more appropriate than word getting out that Derek Murdoch was taking his girlfriend traveling on the taxpayer's dime.

She had to concede. They'd been at the conference for
fourteen hours straight, an exciting and exhausting day, and
they would have the rest of the evening to themselves for
once. Yes, at that moment it was working absolutely.

Derek said, "This is the one thing I don't even want to
analyze. It will wreck the magic of it all. I don't know why it
works, but it does, and can't we enjoy that?"

He'd called it magic. But. "I just want to make sure that
all this is going somewhere," she said. She didn't only mean

whatever was blossoming between them as a couple, the progression of their relationship; she was talking about her life in general. She had finished school and all the other people her age around her were beginning to launch into the stratosphere of adulthood, and there were moments she wondered if she was missing out, tagging along on someone else's business trips. Coattails. Derek had already had years to get where he was going, and what if she was mistaking his momentum for her own? What if one day she woke up and realized that she'd only been standing still?

But Derek would just start kissing her neck, saying "Let's be here now" the way he always did. Just like he did a few weeks later when she was lying in his bed in the city and it was six o'clock in the morning. He'd been out jogging already, was about to get into the shower, and was urging her to take her time, to watch TV. The night table on what she thought of as "her side" was bare. Once she'd dared to leave a tube of hand cream in the drawer, but the next time she'd come over it wasn't there anymore. She never mentioned it again, a failed experiment.

It was a bit early in the day for such an intense discussion regarding the state of their union, but the subject had come up because he'd already told her twice that morning not to hurry. He seemed anxious about this, as though she might expect that the two of them would head in to the office together, conspicuously a couple.

She told him, "Relax. I know my place."

He said, "Don't be like that." They'd been together for almost six months now, and the tension was becoming harder to ignore. Brooke was mostly content to just go with the flow, but it made her uneasy how afraid he seemed of their relationship becoming a spectacle. What did it mean if the worst thing Derek could imagine was people finding out that they were together?

But most of the time, things between them were very good, which is why these spats never went on for long. Because all Derek had to do was get into bed with her, all sweaty and gross, his towel falling on the floor—and this was something, because Derek's condo was pristine. He was a neat freak.

He would say, "What can I possibly do to show you?"

She'd tell him, "Well, there is that."

And while they might not come into the office with their arms around each other, and she still sauntered in in her own good time, she'd get to spend the day with the satisfaction of knowing she was the reason he'd been forty minutes late.

Brooke was well versed in workplace romance, the only kind she'd ever known since coming of age, so she was accustomed to some awkwardness, the tension, and she knew not to bring her personal issues into the office. None of it was that difficult to navigate, and frankly she didn't know how anyone found time for a relationship with a person they didn't see between the hours of nine and five, especially since the day usually stretched much longer than that. She would never have seen Derek at all if she didn't get to be with him at work.

Which wasn't to say that things were always straightforward—when the summer intern reported her crush on
Derek, Brooke had to keep a straight face, and then even
smile kindly. Afterwards, she filled Derek in on the details
with a tip that he should probably be careful. And Brooke
could see how the intern might have gotten the wrong idea
about Derek, because he was a funny, charming guy, the
consummate politician who had a talent for making you feel
like the most important person in the room, and women who
aren't generally subject to that kind of attention from a man
can interpret it as potentially romantic.

"Do you trust him?" Carly had asked Brooke at the very
beginning, when she was still getting the lay of the land.

"Of course I do," said Brooke, and she also knew how
foolish she sounded, how naïve. She remembered that first
summer with Miranda, and also Kelly and Eliza, and all the
summers that came after. But if she didn't trust Derek, she
wouldn't have been with him—she hoped that Carly could
give her enough credit for that. And understand that she
wanted Derek more than she wanted to spend her time clin-
ically examining all the flaws in her judgment. Not everything had to be logical.

So she had to sit back and watch Derek do his thing, creating these wrong impressions, having most of the women
he encountered entertain the notion that he might be in love
with them, because this was how a politician gets elected,
after all. Which sounds terrible, but in comparison to his
counterparts a generation older, with their certainty that

women's minds and bodies were theirs for the taking, Derek really was a gentleman.

Brooke rarely got the best of him, though. After days of listening—to other people's stories, to criticism and abuse, to questions from the other party that were talking points vaguely framed as inquiry, to sad and sorry people who'd never had a person listen to them in all their lives—Derek would come home entirely spent. He couldn't listen anymore, and he didn't want to talk, either. So Brooke would find herself hanging around his house like a redundant appliance, getting in his way, and eventually she learned that there were some nights when it was just better that she go back to her place. She knew not to take it personally.

Other than while traveling, their best times were arriving back to his condo together at the end of the day, both of them exhausted, but excited and inspired by what their team had accomplished. She'd helped write a speech he'd delivered with aplomb on the floor, or else a long-planned event had gone off without a hitch. These were days when it felt like they were partners, both in life and something larger. Like when they used to go out running together, except that she'd managed to keep the pace.

There were precious stolen moments—a few weekends at his house back home when they got to spend all day in their pajamas, reading the papers together. Before Derek, Brooke had always gotten her news online, but he taught her the value in ink on your fingers, the charm of unfolding the sheets of paper and reading with both arms flung out wide.

And she loved being in the car with him, no matter where they were going. Zero distractions, except for music on the radio. He said she made an excellent travel companion, and he started having her assigned on all his trips. He got nervous flying, and he'd squeeze her hand. He told her, "I love going anywhere with you."

But then they'd arrive and get off the plane, get out of the car, and things between them would once again become formal. She liked to brush the shoulders of his suits just to touch him, and then she'd stand back in the crowd watching him in action. Thinking about how nobody else in the room knew that he was hers—but they also thought he was all theirs, so she wasn't sure it counted.

"You're really happy with all this?" all the people who purported to love her would demand.

Her friends organized a night out for her birthday, but Derek would not be attending. "They're all so hostile about us," he said. "You'll have a better time without me there."

He had tried to win them over at first, the way he won over everybody, but his tricks weren't as effective on those whose concerns were that he was like a politician, in the worst way. They thought he was smarmy, because they didn't know him like she did.

"He only tells you what you want to hear," said Nicole, before Nicole gave up on being critical of the relationship because she feared her criticism was driving Brooke away from her, which it was.

Carly showed less restraint: "I know Derek Murdoch," she said. She didn't trust him at all. "This is his pattern."

And Brooke had no proof to offer that it wasn't, except that she knew with all her heart that it was different this time, which was evidence enough. Or should have been— for real friends. She was adamant about that, so she began to see these friends less often.

And then, of course, Derek would show up on the cover of magazines with profiles focusing on his personal life, and one calling him "the city's most eligible bachelor," and she was furious about that one. And then, finally, for once in her life, Brooke lost her cool.

"You called yourself 'eligible'?" They were in his office with the door closed. The story had just gone online that day, and someone had printed out the photo and pinned it to the noticeboard, hearts drawn along the borders in pink highlighter.

He said, "I didn't call myself anything. You know how it goes. They've got to come up with a headline."

"It makes me look bad," Brooke said.

"In the eyes of who?" he asked.

"Me," she answered, "and don't tell me that doesn't matter. That it doesn't count. It's not fair to just dismiss me."

He said, "You know that these things aren't up to me, right? What they write in magazines? And what do you want me to do about it? You knew this was how it was going to be—exactly like this. You're the one here who has a choice in how things go."

"You mean, like take it or leave it?" said Brooke. "Because I don't know that's such a choice." What she wanted was for there to be some space in which she could retain the smallest bit of agency, where maybe her feelings and needs could be a priority, but a person only gets to own that space when they're dating ordinary people, and when your boyfriend is the city's most eligible bachelor, compromise becomes a necessary requirement.

"It's possible to bend over backwards so far that you become a human doormat," Nicole wrote once in an email Brooke never replied to.

She told Derek now, "You only hold my hand when there's no one around."

"But that's not you, it's just how things are. You know we've got to keep it on the down-low."

She said, "But would it really be so bad if people knew? That's the part that really bothers me—I don't know which one you're scared of more: the word getting out, or losing me altogether. Or maybe the problem is that I do."

"I don't want to lose you," he said. "You know it's not like that."

"But no, really," she said. "What if you had to choose one?"

"Come on."

"I mean it," she said.

He said, "What, like extortion?"

"See, that's my point," she said. "It's not like extortion. It's about giving me the respect I deserve."

"I don't think that blackmail," he said, "is particularly respectful."

"I'm not blackmailing you," she said, exasperated, and then she lowered her voice. "I'm making a point. It's on principle. Just think about it. Just think about what it means that the idea of me telling the world about us makes you so terrified."

"I'm not terrified," he said. He was nervous, though— she could see it. He took a deep breath and tried to soften his tone. "If I could, I would give you everything you wanted." It was the closest he'd ever come to promising her anything.

She said, "But that means nothing, really. In the end."

Derek got up from his desk and walked over to the glass walls and closed the blinds, shutting out their colleagues on the other side. Turning back around, he got down on his knee before her and took her hand. What was he doing? "Come on, you know what the terms are. We've got to be realistic."

Brooke said, "They let other politicians have personal lives."

He said, "It's complicated. You know that better than anyone. That's why it works with us, because you get it, how it is."

"But I don't have to like it."

"I never asked you to like it. I don't like it either." She was still wondering why he was kneeling on the floor. Anyone walking in and seeing them there would think he was pro- posing, and even though she knew that he wasn't, that he wouldn't, just the possibility of creating such an impression had its own particular romance. "And I don't want to hurt you," he said. "Maybe if all this is hurting you, the logical thing to do would be to call it off. But I don't want to do that. I really don't."

"Me neither," she said.

"And what's been so amazing about all of this anyway," he told her, "has been watching it all unfolding. It's taken years, and it's happened slowly. Going from colleagues, to friends, to this."

"To this."

"Right?"

"But I mean, what is it? This. What are you going to call it?"

"Do we have to call it anything?"

"I think we do."

"You have to call a thing a thing to know what it is?"

"That's not unreasonable," she said. "A definition."

"Definitions are limits," Derek said. "It's all they are. And I hate that."

"But definitions are also what gives something its substance," Brooke said. "And I think that I deserve that."

"Of course you do."

"And I deserve to, just say, be able to count on you, on this. To call what we've got here a relationship—without the world ending, even. I really don't think that would be so unfair." They'd been together for months. She'd known him for years. She wondered if he'd think it was juvenile, her insistence on guiding their relationship in this direction, marking off all the clichéd milestones along the way. She aspired to be more original than that, but she also needed some orientation.

He told her, "You know you make me feel like the luckiest guy in the world, right? I don't know that there is a higher thing to shoot for than the esteemed affection of somebody like you."

"Esteemed affection? That's what we're calling it now?" But he had made her smile.

He said, "You're the one who said we had to call it something."

"I need to know that this is serious. That I'm not wasting my time."

"I don't waste time," said Derek. "My own, or anybody else's. You know that." And then he put his arms around her shoulders and pulled her down so that she was kneeling beside him on the floor, and he kissed her. He said, "I'm going to do whatever I can to make this easier on you."

"You could start by taking the photo down. And I don't care that it makes it look like you can't take a joke. I honestly can't take this joke. Even if nobody knows. It's disrespectful."

"It's disrespectful," he repeated. "I'll take it down."

She said, "I don't want to be a human doormat."

"You're not a doormat," he said.

"I just wonder if it would be easier for you if we didn't do this. If you didn't have to hide. Because you also have a choice here. This isn't all on me."

He said, "You think losing you would be easy?"

"I don't even know what's what."

"I'd be wrecked," he said. "If you walked away from me."

"But another girl would come along," she told him, shrugging her shoulders like this was no big thing. "They always do."

"You aren't 'another girl,'" he said. "You've never been. Haven't I been clear about that?"

"You haven't been clear about much," she said. "Definitions are limits, remember?"

And then he sat back, and leaned against his desk, looking small and totally drained. "You really don't get it?" He looked baffled. "Because I thought we had an understanding."

"I thought the basis of our understanding was that we didn't talk about our understanding."

"Because it didn't need to be said," he told her. "But maybe it did."

"Maybe it did?"

"You know I don't go around falling in love with just anyone."

In love.

"You're really going to make me spell this out?"

"It might be necessary."

"Oh, man," he said. "Brooke, it's never been like this for me. Never. And so many times it would have been easier if a girl walked away, because it's hard to make other people understand. But not this time. This right now, you and me, is the easiest, most straightforward thing. I don't even have to try and make it make sense, because we just click."

"We click?"

"Don't you get it?"

"I do."

"And I don't know, maybe you click with everyone. Maybe you and Trevor—"

She said, "Don't talk about Trevor."

"Mr. Frosted Tips."

"I swear, I will smack you with a stapler."

He said, "No, I'm being serious. For me, it's never been the easiest thing, being in a relationship, making it work. It's always been so hard, everything out of sync. There's so much I want to do, and it's hard to get all the priorities aligned, but with you it's just there. It's the most amazing thing. We wake up in the morning, and there you are. It's as simple as that."

She said, "Kind of like a doormat."

He said, "No. Doormats don't talk." She started to say something smart in response, but he interrupted her. "And I love it when you talk. I love it when you argue, or ask questions, and tell me things that I don't know, which is a lot of the time. I love it when you edit my speeches, and tell me jokes, and when you laugh at my jokes." He was getting up on his knees again, and they were face to face. He reached out and placed his finger in the dip between her breasts, her blouse open to the third button. He said, "And doormats are flat. You're not flat." He kissed her. Murmured, "I love you, Brooke Ellis. It's not even hypothetical. Or theoretical."

She was sitting there with the dumbest smile on her face—she could feel it there, hanging, big and goofy. From the incredible lightness of all her patience and faith being rewarded. And she told him, "One day you're going to kiss me when the blinds aren't shut." It was really going to happen. Derek needed her, and there was nobody else who knew him the way that she did.

So she believed him when he put his hand on his heart and said, "I promise."

———

They took their relationship to the next level after that, which meant their colleagues knew, and when she accompanied him on trips, they stopped booking her a separate hotel room. It also meant that all conversations would end abruptly every time she walked into the lunchroom, however. But sometimes when other people were around, Derek held her hand, or else he'd rub her shoulders as he leaned over her desk to see what she was getting up to.

And there were whispers, rumors, posts on social media and shady political blogs, but Derek insisted that it didn't freak him out. "If it gets out, it gets out," he said. He was attempting the posture of a person who really was that cool, but Brooke had been the one to see him, a quivering mess kneeling on his office floor with the blinds shut. So even though he was almost convincing, she saw through it all the same, but the effort he put into the act, into trying to be strong, only made her love him even more, and she told him so. She admired the way he buried his fears for her, for them. That she mattered to him enough to do that, which should have been enough to convince Carly, Nicole, and everyone.

He didn't tell his family, though. He said it would be too hard. "They'd be all over you then," he told her. "And you don't want that." Even though he was so close to his family— they still took vacations together, and celebrated birthdays, and holidays. Derek's official Christmas cards every year featured a photo of all of them, his parents, his sisters, his nephews, brothers-in-law, and his ninety-six-year-old grandma. They were a huge part of his life—his mom visited the office all the time and Brooke had been introduced to her on several occasions, although she'd never had reason to set Brooke apart from the gaggle of women in Derek's employ.

His parents were old-fashioned, he said. His sisters hadn't even lived with their husbands before they got married. Derek loved his mother, but she could be too much, and expectations were high after all these years of them waiting for Derek to bring someone special home. "I don't want you to have to deal with all of that until you have to."

But at least they were finally talking about a future. After the election, perhaps, they could make things official. Derek was nervous, because, he said, when he was serious about a relationship, he was serious. "I want to get married," he said. "There's no messing around." And Brooke was still so young. "I want to make sure you're ready too," he told her. "It's going to be for a lifetime when it happens, so we don't need to rush to get there. And I don't want you to miss anything before then."

"The one thing I really don't want to miss is you," she told him. They were driving up north for the long weekend— he'd spent a lot of time back in his office in Lanark that summer while the government was on break, and for once this time he'd brought her with him. She hadn't told her parents she was coming home, because she didn't plan to see them. This weekend was about the two of them, the kind of moments Derek had been making a point of since that day in the office with the blinds shut. There weren't any groceries at his place, but she'd stopped at the bakery and picked out a box full of pastries. She was determined to prove it was possible to live on love and chocolate doughnuts alone.

"Provisions," she told him, when he came to get her at her desk. She hadn't had anything to do all day—she'd just been waiting.

And he'd said, "That's the only drawback to being with someone half your age. The metabolism. You're turning me into a flabby old man, Brooke." And she delighted in the idea she had any power over him at all, even though she knew it was nonsense. Derek had the willpower of a triathlete, because he was one, simply mind over matter. That weekend she'd end up eating all the pastries, and he'd just subsist on air.

But that weekend would turn out to be another weekend where things didn't go according to plan, when the world interrupted them, this time in the form of Brent Ames and the rest of Derek's buddies, none of whom Brooke could ever tell apart and some of whom had teenage daughters who were closer to Brooke's age than they were, rolling up the long driveway with cases of beer and shouting chants as they drank, which only got louder as they got drunker. She spent the evening in Derek's bedroom eating doughnuts, and he never came to bed.

Friday Evening

Is she making a case here? A case for her and Derek, and what they were together, that it meant anything at all? A case that would make someone more convinced than her friends had been, or the girls in their office who'd stopped inviting her out for drinks with them? All that Brooke can offer are these shining moments that, in her memory, are always golden, cast in amber. Like Derek's hand in her hand as they were on the road to somewhere. Nobody else will ever know how it felt, the firmness of his grip. Like an anchor, but holding her fast, not in the sense of pulling her down.

They couldn't have understood, though, her friends, whose own boyfriends had only ever been boys with whom they'd trod the well-worn path of courtship, with all its milestones and clichés. Why couldn't her friends understand why somebody might want something different from that, as rewarding as it was risky? They had no idea what it meant to be in a relationship where the stakes were high, where what happened really mattered and didn't just crib the plot of another teen romance. "You're not even properly living your lives," is what Brooke thought when she had to listen to her friends lecture her on the chances she was taking with Derek and the mistakes she was making, while they were only ever reciting lines and playing parts. They always knew exactly what was going to happen next, because it was only what was happening to everyone, and that was a life that held no appeal to Brooke, even if the choices she was making were so much harder. No matter how straightforward it was, she and Derek on the road to somewhere, everything between them working—but it was always more complicated upon arrival. Somebody's phone was buzzing, an urgent message, a change of plans. Life is never simple, and a political life, a public one, was even less so, but this was also what Brooke loved about it, the unexpectedness, how it was never boring. She had friends who talked about being bored at work, but she was never bored at her job, or in her relationship, either. It all felt as miraculous as it had from the very start, every day bringing with it something new, another wrench sometimes, but she knew how to deal with those, with the challenges. Brooke was good at what she did.

"You can't possibly be happy with this," were Nicole's exact words the final time she tried to articulate her concerns about her sister's relationship, but Brooke was happy.

She really had been. And that should have been enough, and anybody else's opinion on the subject, even Nicole's, really didn't matter.

All afternoon in the quiet library Brooke had been itemizing amber moments of her and Derek together—she'd made a mental spreadsheet, because she didn't want any of it to get lost. Remembering what Nicole had said: "You can't possibly be happy." The phone call on the night of the press conference had been the first conversation she'd had with her sister in a long time. She'd barely seen her since moving back to Lanark, their schedules out of sync just so subtly so that their parents had hardly noticed their estrangement, but Brooke was sure Nicole knew the reason for their distance.

And now here was Nicole, walking into the library, as though Brooke had conjured her.

"So this is it," said Nicole, looking around the library. "The big chance you uprooted your whole life back in the city for." This was exactly why Brooke had been avoiding Nicole, because she insisted on telling it like it was—or at least like how she perceived it to be, which to Nicole would always be the same thing. She saw the look on Brooke's face, though, and tempered her comment. "I just never pictured you here. I still can't. I used to bring you here when you were three. It doesn't look right, like you're sitting in someone else's chair."

"Well, it's been my chair since the summer," said Brooke. "Whether you can picture it or not. What are you doing here?" Nicole's arrival would be no accident. She was a busy woman, running her business, married to her high school sweetheart, her whole life a perfect arrangement, right down to the pickets in her fence. The one potential sore point in this perfect arrangement being that they hadn't had children. She'd always wanted to, and Nicole had never said why it hadn't happened. Other people's internal affairs were always Nicole's business, but she didn't like to talk about her own.

She said, "Mom told me to come."

"Did she."

"And I had to pick up a few things in town anyway. Believe me, not everything revolves around you." If only that were true. "And I told her you wouldn't want to see me, that I'd only be intruding, but she made me do it. She's more worried than usual. What happened?"

"To who?"

"To you. She said you're hiding. And I said, 'So it's not just me,' and she said it wasn't. And now all this garbage about Derek. You're so mysterious about everything that went down between the two of you, and Mom knows even less than I do, but she doesn't think you should be alone right now. So I've come to take you to dinner."

"I'm working."

"For ten more minutes," she said. "I know your schedule."

"I might have plans," said Brooke.

"Mom said you never have plans."

"Mom doesn't know everything about me," said Brooke. "And neither do you."

"So you do have plans?" Nicole asked.

Brooke admitted, "No." She was still waiting to hear from Derek. She wanted to be ready to jump into a cab and be out at his place at a moment's notice—so no, this was not a great time for dinner. But Brooke couldn't tell her sister that, because it would only prove Nicole's point, the one she kept returning to, which was that Brooke was being undone by everything, that Derek's downfall was becoming her own.

Brooke said, "You don't have to do this. And what's Sean doing tonight?"

"Sean is pretty good at fending for himself," said Nicole. "And it's definitely time for a catch-up anyway, you and me. I've even missed you, a little bit. As I've mentioned. And I've been worried." She gestured toward the periodicals, at the papers hung that morning with Derek still on the front page. Looking more polished, but wan under the headline:

GIRLS "NOT YOUNG. NEVER UNDERAGE."

Things still weren't looking good. Nicole said, "I'll wait over here."

She sat at the table by the papers and watched Brooke on her perch at the counter doing nothing. She didn't even bother to pick up a magazine, some kind of distraction. She just stared at Brooke as she went through the motions of the end of her shift, shutting down terminals, putting up chairs, and turning out lights. She'd already made an announcement that the library was closing in fifteen minutes, and now it was time for the five-minute call. She got on the PA system and cleared her throat like a warning, so she wouldn't startle remaining patrons too badly.

"The library will be closing in five minutes," she said smoothly into the speaker. "Please bring your materials to be signed out to the circulation desk."

But there was nobody left, as Lindsay confirmed when she came back up from her sweep of the stacks with Peter the Security Guard. He saw Nicole waiting. "A friend of yours?" he asked Brooke.

Brooke said, "Peter, do you remember my sister?"

"He likes you," Nicole said afterwards over sushi, which wouldn't have been Brooke's first choice for dinner because the sushi in this town was not incredible, but the only alternative was the Italian place, and when your father owns the pizza joint, going there would be disloyal. So sushi it was, sashimi even, which Nicole ordered because she was the kind of vegetarian where fish was fine, although her choice confirmed she definitely still wasn't pregnant, and she must have been studying the expression on Brooke's face as this occurred to her, but she got the reading all wrong.

"And yes, Ms. City Slicker, we've got sashimi out here in the boonies."

"I live here," Brooke reminded her sister, before Nicole went all-in accusing her of snobbery.

"But you don't really," she said. "It's like Mom said. You're hiding. And not just from me, but from everything. I want to find out what's going on. Is this about Derek? What a mess."

What if Brooke just told Nicole everything? What if she just came out with the whole story, a burden lifted? She would have her sister back again, because did she really have to be so alone in this? It would be so easy; it would feel so good. But she couldn't do it. Not yet. Everything was still hinging on what Derek would have to tell her tonight.

"It's not true," Brooke told her. "What they're saying."

"That Derek Murdoch goes out with girls who work for him, girls just out of school? Sound familiar?"

Brooke asked, "Since when is that illegal?" The waitress delivered their miso soup. Brooke had never been in a Japanese restaurant before where all the staff were white. "And no, I mean the other stuff."

"How he made some poor girl suck him off in a trash can."

"It wasn't like that," said Brooke.

"You were there?"

"I know him," said Brooke. "He wouldn't do that. Besides, it was a long time ago."

"That doesn't mean it never happened."

"You're being unfair," Brooke told her sister. And not for the first time.

"The whole thing gives me a bad vibe," Nicole had confessed to Brooke back when she and Derek first got together, and now Brooke could see from her sister's expression that the vibe hadn't changed since then.

"So Derek's still your hero?" she said to Brooke now. "Even after all those things they're saying?"

"People say things all the time. Doesn't mean they're true."

"I'm still curious about why he packed you off home, though. What happened?"

"He didn't pack me anywhere."

"You're still seeing him?"

Brooke said, "It's complicated."

"It's probably less complicated than you think," Nicole said. "Have you seen him lately?"

Not since she left the city in June. "He's coming home this weekend," Brooke told her.

Nicole said, "Of course he is. He's got his tail between his legs. Among other things."

"He'll be back tonight. I'm waiting to hear from him." Her phone was on the table, and she'd had to move it aside to make room when the food arrived.

Nicole said, "I'm worried about you too, you know. It's not just Mom being crazy. It's like you're disappearing."

Brooke said, "I'm right here."

"But not really," said Nicole. "And what are you doing here anyway? It doesn't make any sense. You're better than all this, don't you know that? Better than small-town sushi, even. Don't think I don't know that. You're fooling no one. Something's up."

"I just needed a break," said Brooke.

Nicole leveled with her. "It's like you're broken. And I don't know if it was him who did this to you, but it makes me furious. You're my little sister."

"I'm twenty-three years old," said Brooke. "What makes you think that anyone did anything to me?"

"What does age have to do with any of it?"

"Because you're treating me like a child."

"I'm not. We'd be having this conversation no matter how old you were. You also don't have to pretend to be invulnerable, you know. Being a human being is nothing to be ashamed of."

"I'm not ashamed." Her phone buzzed—it was him. The sweet relief of her faith rewarded again. The world righted on its axis. She was not such a fool after all. *Can you call me? Tonight?*

She texted back, *I'm out for dinner. Hang on. Soon.*

"So that's him?" Brooke nodded. "And you're going over there? He's coming to pick you up?" His place was way out of town, inaccessible by public transit. She could take a taxi.

"He just got home," said Brooke. "It's been a long drive. I can't ask him to come all the way downtown."

"But you shouldn't have to ask him, Brooke," said Nicole. "That's just my point."

"You don't understand."

Nicole said, "I do. Just because a person has a job that's important doesn't mean they're obligated to treat everyone around them like crap."

"He doesn't do that," said Brooke.

Nicole said, "I'll drive you, once we're finished here."

Brooke said, "It's out of your way."

"But see, that's what we do for the people we love," her sister said. "We go out of our way. We come downtown. We remind them at every single turn that they are essential, incredible, valuable parts of our lives." She made it sound so easy.

"How *is* Sean?" Brooke asked. Sean was like that. He was as reliable as his pick-up truck.

"Sean's good," said Nicole. "You don't need to stay away, you know. You've moved back up here, and I see you less than when you were in the city."

Brooke said, "It's not been the best time."

"I know," said Nicole. She squeezed Brooke's hand across the table. "You're wasting an incredible resource, though, a big sister who is willing to beat the living daylights out of anyone who'd dare to hurt you. I swear, if you want me to nail his dick to the wall, I'd do it."

"Nicole!" said Brooke. "What would Maria Montessori think?" But she was smiling now, the idea of Nicole wielding a hammer in rage. She said, "But you don't have to do that. I can take care of myself. And nobody has hurt me— it's just complicated. Like I said."

"Uh-huh," she said, and rolled her eyes.

Brooke's phone buzzed.

"Is it him?" Nicole asked.

We need to talk, he'd written. This moment she'd been waiting months for, beginning to fear it might never come. Finally she had a leg to stand on, a shred of dignity. She hadn't been wrong about everything.

Brooke nodded. It was him.

And Nicole said, "I'll take you there."

Brooke hadn't been out to Derek's place since coming back to town, except for one time when her mom had loaned her the car to go buy towels and bed linen at Walmart, and she'd just kept going beyond the boundary line where the town turned into country and the road became a highway. She'd known where she was heading without even thinking about it, that line from an old song running through her head about driving by a house even though you know that no one's home.

But she had wanted to see it, that house that was his, a place that had felt like *theirs* more than once or twice. And of course, the house was all locked up because Derek was back in the city, and Brooke didn't have a key, which underlined that this house had never been theirs at all. Perhaps nothing had been. She hadn't even slowed down at the end of the driveway, because she didn't want the neighbors noticing, or people thinking she was insane.

But the windows at the front were glowing now, and Derek's car was parked by the kitchen door. And nobody else's car was there, which was what she hadn't been sure of. *I'll be back tonight*, he'd texted. *We need to connect.* Inside that house, he was waiting for her.

"You can stop here," she said to Nicole, even though they were only partway up the driveway. She didn't want

Nicole's presence to complicate things—she might be hiding a hammer in her purse. And here there was still enough room for her to turn the car around. To go.

Nicole said, "I could wait for you. Just to make sure he's home."

"His car's right there," Brooke said.

She said, "It just seems really quiet."

Brooke said, "I think it's been a long week."

"He knows you're coming?"

"He asked me."

"I've got my phone," said Nicole. She patted her purse on the console between them. "Call me, and I can come right back and get you."

"But you're going back in the other direction," said Brooke.

Nicole shrugged. It didn't matter.

She was turned around watching Nicole drive away, because she wanted to make sure that she was really going, going, gone. She knew Nicole's eyes were on the rearview watching Brooke all the way, so Brooke stood still and waited, and it was only once the car had disappeared down the road that she turned back around, and there he was on the side porch. He must've heard the car. He was smaller than life, which was what she always thought after not having seen him in a while, and this was the longest she'd been away from him since they'd met more than five years before. A quarter of her conscious existence. She'd almost forgotten that he was real, that he could just be standing there wearing an old blue sweater she recognized with the sleeves stretched out too long. Finally, they were where they were supposed to be, and she suppressed an urge to rush toward him and reach out and touch him, to hold him, holding back instead, sensing his hesitation, some discomfort. The look on his face, how his lips were pulled thin. It had been so long. She walked slowly instead.

"What are you doing here?" he asked, coming down the steps. "Whose car was that? How did you get here?" He sounded panicked, paranoid. Something wasn't right.

She wanted to stop him and his string of questions, to reassure him. "It's only me," she said. But he was waiting for her answers. "The car's my sister's," Brooke told him, her voice deliberately calm. "She gave me a ride." What was she missing here? What exactly was he so afraid of?

He said, "I don't get it." Asking the question again, "What are you doing here?" As though he hadn't been expecting her.

But he'd told her to come. "You wanted to talk."

"On the *phone*," he said. No, snapped. He could be mean, she knew he could be mean. He could be cruel, when he felt cornered. When he had been drinking. He didn't come any closer, and Brooke stayed still, not because she felt threatened, but because she didn't want to have to see him start to inch away from her. The old-fashioned word popped into her head again: *besmirch*. But why did she feel like she was the one who'd been besmirched now?

She said, "I didn't realize." Still calm. She'd been trained in dealing with unstable clients at the library, and this felt just like that. She didn't want to set him off. No sudden moves. What had happened?

"This isn't good," he said. "Who else knows you're here?"

"Just Nicole," she said. "Listen, can't I come in? I thought we could talk."

"This isn't good," he said again. "Not good at all. And how are you supposed to get back?"

She'd barely arrived. "You could drive me," she suggested. The simplest solution. Did she really have to go?

He said, "I can't do that. And you can't call a taxi—those guys talk." He wasn't wrong about that. The taxi dispatch was right next door to her dad's pizza place.

Brooke thought of Nicole's promise to come back and get her, but that would only compound her humiliation. Nicole didn't need to be involved.

She took a chance. "Are you okay?" she asked him. "What's the big deal? I mean, I've been here before."

"This is different," he said.

"Because of what happened? This week?" Derek was the first person she'd spoken to who she didn't need to convince of Derek's innocence, the only person who knew better than she did. You might have thought this would be a relief, some kind of alliance, but clearly Brooke had missed something along the way.

"The paper," said Derek. "You've heard from the paper? The reporter said she was trying to reach you."

"Shondra Decker. I got her emails."

"You didn't—"

"But it's okay," she told him, finally understanding. She started walking toward him again. His sleeves were so long, stretched, and he was clinging to them. He was anxious, in a really bad way. She could recognize when he got like this, and she also knew that when he was, she could be the one to make him calm.

But he said, "Stop." He stepped away from her. "You don't get it," he said. "Everything's on the line."

"But what does it matter now?" she asked him. "Nobody else is here."

He said, "No, you can't be here. That reporter."

Brooke repeated, "But it's okay. I talked to her."

"You talked to her."

"I told her that you were one of the good guys."

"But it wasn't just a story about me," he told Brooke. "That reporter—she was writing about you."

"DEREK MURDOCH: COMPLICATED OR NOT, HE'S THE REAL THING"

WHEN HE WON THE leadership race two years ago, Derek Murdoch's name was unfamiliar to most of the voting public who, along with all the pundits, had been expecting the position to go to long-time politician Joan Dunn. Dunn had spent twenty-one years serving in three levels of government and brought considerable expertise and experience to the table.

"But what else I brought," admitted Dunn in the race's aftermath, "was baggage." The party had been riven by years of infighting and frustrated by almost two decades of disappointing election results. "It really was the perfect moment for a sea change, and Derek Murdoch seized it. To be honest, we didn't even see him coming."

To anyone who knew Murdoch and was aware of his history, however, the victory seemed predestined. "He's been doing incredible things right out of the gate," explains political strategist Phil Phelps. "When he's given a challenge or a proposition, Derek never wavers or asks 'Why?' or 'How?' He just gets down to work and says, 'Let's make this happen.' And now he's done it again."

It wasn't all smooth sailing, though. It didn't sit well in progressive circles that this young upstart—who called himself "demonstrably a feminist"—had just unseated a female politician with decades of experience under her belt. It was a tricky place to be, although others pointed out that true equality was a man and a woman challenging each other on a level playing field, and to suggest Dunn should have been treated differently than other politicians was to undermine everything that made her deserving of the leadership at all.

There were also whispers about the membership drives that possibly delivered Murdoch his victory—he is well connected with local businesses that enticed newbie party members with booze and barbeques. There were reports of raucous behavior at nightclubs and pool parties, and an old photo surfaced of Murdoch with his arm around the shoulders of a topless woman, her bikini in his other hand as he twirls it like a lasso. It suggested the kind of scandal that most politicians would never recover from, but the woman came forward, unabashed, saying she's an old friend of Murdoch's, and they were only having fun. She was furious that any paper might publish the image.

The other problem for Murdoch with feminism is his stance on abortion, which he insists is nuanced. He grew up in a religious family with strict anti-abortion views, and members of his family's church back in his hometown of Lanark are notorious for holding gory protests with dismembered baby dolls outside the local hospital where abortions take place. Murdoch is fast to distance himself from these displays—"I don't think it's fair to judge an entire congregation by the actions of a handful," he says. He also reminds critics that he left that congregation as a teenager because of his discomfort with their hard lines on social issues, abortion included.

"I knew that point of view did not gel with the reality of women's lives," he explains. He wanted no part of a system working to restrict a woman's reproductive choice. And yet, on a personal level, he doesn't call himself pro-choice. "I just can't," he says. "It wouldn't be honest. And I could sit here and lie to you, and tell you I'm just fine with it—it would be convenient if I could, you know?—but it wouldn't mean anything. And I think we need to mean what we say—it's the point of everything."

He explains that he grew up in a culture that taught that all life is sacred. "And they weren't wrong about that," he says. "I still believe that to the core of my being, which is why I do the things I do. It's why we support addicts and recovery, it's why we want to introduce a universal basic income to alleviate poverty, it's why school breakfast programs matter, and why people need good and safe jobs to be able to support their families. It's why I spearheaded sexual health programs for at-risk youth almost twenty years ago. Because every life is precious. And I'm not going to ever be the one to draw a line between those that are worthy and the ones that fall outside that jurisdiction."

He is adamant that he's not interested in reopening a debate on abortion and would never use his political power for that purpose. "This is business between a woman and her doctor, and it's got nothing to do with me. But I'm also not going to stand up here and tell you I'm pro-choice, that I'm just cool with it and don't find abortion to be morally troubling as an issue."

It's a stance that doesn't sit well with other demonstrable feminists. Earlier this year, activist Tanya Major of abortion-rights group Women for Choice started an online petition calling for Murdoch's resignation unless he issues a statement in support of abortion rights. But others understand and even admire the thoughtfulness of his perspective.

"It's a huge part of his appeal," says his colleague Cindy Atwell, who was elected at the same time and has served with Murdoch on many committees. "He's the real thing, and real doesn't always mean 'easy.' Real doesn't always work in soundbites or in 140 characters, but it's genuine, and that resonates with people. Even if you don't agree with him—and with this, I don't agree with him—but I respect his point of view."

The challenges that lie before Derek Murdoch now are about more than just capturing hearts. He is charged with repairing the divisions in his party after a particularly fractious leadership race, and then with winning over voters in a population that's becoming more and more polarized all the time. What kind of a place is there for Murdoch's socialist-based policies in this charged political atmosphere?

But Derek Murdoch will not be daunted. "Over my years in politics," he says, "I've heard again and again that it can't be done, but it's all a matter of connecting with people and understanding that there's a reasonable way to do things that takes into account how people really live and what they need. Nobody wants to live in the world so bitter and angry. There's a place where those emotions are coming from, and if you really understand that, if you really listen, people are willing to open their minds up in return. I've learned to never give up on the amazing possibilities of people working together."

Saturday Morning

Brooke didn't look for the article online, because she knew she would find it in the paper in the morning, waiting on her parents' doorstep. Rolled up, secured with an elastic, and she steeled herself as she picked it up to read the headline on display. A story not quite sensational enough for all-capital letters, but still larger than usual, clearly conveying something worthy of attention:

DEREK MURDOCH'S GIRLFRIEND SAYS HE'S "ONE OF THE GOOD GUYS"

And underneath it, once she'd removed the elastic and unrolled the bundle, a photo of her and Derek wearing tacky Hawaiian shirts from this one night everybody had gone bowling for somebody's birthday. His arm around her shoulders and they were smiling. Brooke looked like she was falling-over drunk, because she had been. Other people had been cropped out of the shot, she realized, so it looked like just the two of them, an ordinary image of a couple laughing. She didn't have a single picture of them like this. Not long after her relationship with Derek had become known in the office, she'd had to go through her social media and scrub all the photos where Derek appeared, no matter that her privacy settings were so high that no one would have been able to see them anyway.

And so her first reaction to the image, to the headline even, was a rush of tenderness. Because how much time had she spent longing for precisely what she saw on that page, above the fold, even? To be Derek's girlfriend, posing laughing in photos for everyone to see. Imagining people picking up the paper and seeing this image made her feel marginally less humiliated than she'd felt in months. It was the opposite of the night before, when she'd been driven home from Derek's house by Kirsti Ames, his best friend Brent's youngest sister.

Kirsti was three years older than she was, and Brooke remembered her from school, although Kirsti didn't know Brooke. She didn't know what Brooke was doing at Derek's, either, or that she'd ever meant something to him—that she wasn't just another of his hangers-on, the kind of girl he used to pick up at the bars downtown.

Brooke was crying in the passenger seat as Kirsti turned out of the driveway. Once she was on the road, she pulled a wad of tissues out of the pocket of her hoodie and told her, "Hey, I don't know what all this is about, but I promise you it's not worth getting so upset about. He's just a boy, like all of them. They're never not going to break your heart, but they're certainly not worth crying about."

Brooke took a deep breath and recovered her senses, then told her, "Yeah, well, you don't know."

Kirsti said, "I bet I do, though. I've known these guys my whole life—Derek, my brother. And it's always the same story. Some people don't have to ever grow up."

Brooke said, "It's not like that. He's not like that. There's his job—"

"Oh, right," said Kirsti. "His *job*. Which gives him a reason to put on a nice suit, and the means to afford it, and suddenly people are taking him seriously now. But it's superficial. All of it is. Same with my brother."

"You don't like your brother?"

"I love my brother," said Kirsti. They were driving back into town, cheap motels popping up on either side of the highway alongside discount shoe outlets and auto repair shops. "But I wouldn't advise anyone to go out with him, or marry him. Any of his friends, either. They're like the Lost Boys, all of them. And all these women imagining they'll be able to rescue one of them or another. It never works. They only end up crying."

"I'm not crying," said Brooke, determined to stop.

"Well, good," said Kirsti. "That's a start. Don't waste another minute of your time crying over somebody like him. You're better than that."

"I don't know about that."

Kirsti said, "*Everybody* is better than that." She turned onto the main drag. "Now where are we going?" She really didn't know anything. Derek had phoned Brent, who'd called his sister, who didn't know what Brooke was doing at his place, or where she was supposed to take her.

Brooke gave directions to her parents' house, because she needed to be the one to break this news before they found out in the morning. And also because this would be a night, she knew, where it would help to be less lonely.

BEFORE

When you are twenty-three, and your boyfriend is thirty-eight, there is a great deal of pressure not to seem childish, or *teenaged*. Like, you shouldn't even call him your boyfriend, for that matter, because "boyfriend" is adolescent, and if he ever overheard himself referred to as such (like, say, when you're on the phone to a lingerie store asking about the exchange policy on a birthday gift he bought you that was two sizes too small and which he hadn't saved a receipt for), he'd raise the matter with you afterwards, leaving you feeling stupid, embarrassed, diminished.

"This isn't high school, Brooke," is something he'd remind you of a couple of times, and then ever after you'd hear the phrase in your head, never mind that you hadn't been in high school yourself for years. Maybe there were even things you knew about adulthood that he had not yet begun to master, such as flossing, the basics of bicycle repair, buying his own shirts, and when it was time to start shopping for his nephews' birthdays.

But you can't press him on these points, because pressing back would only underline what you have been hearing from all sides, which is that you have a tendency toward childishness, to become hysterical, and there is much about the world you can't possibly know yet. It's not that he thinks you are stupid, or even annoying. In fact he just finds you completely adorable, and he loves your innocence, your energy, your willingness to engage with or consider new and wild ideas. Your freshness—he loves your freshness. You are spontaneous and up for anything. Unlike the women his age, who have already begun to wilt. Together you and he are unhappy for those women, all their petals falling off. You are in your fullest bloom, and he begins to command this performance. He doesn't like you when you're any other way.

Which makes it difficult on the days when you're not up to performing, when you're feeling nauseous and your head hurts, and you're so tired that you curl up on the floor in the stationery cupboard and nap among the Post-its and file folders. Inconvenient enough, but also Brooke's period was late—or, rather, it was missing altogether, because it had been two months since she'd last seen it. And she was working hard not to turn this into yet another crisis, just another excuse to be accused of acting like a child. Late periods were a thing, and it would turn out fine. She was on the pill, which was ninety-something percent effective, and she'd never been enough of an outlier in any respect to run afoul of those odds. The online pregnancy quizzes she kept taking were inconclusive—it could be mono, or influenza, and there was still a chance it would turn out to be cancer.

Mostly, though, Brooke was trying to ignore it, when she wasn't sleeping among the Post-it notes. They were busy at work, and her schedule was crazy, so it was easy to be distracted and think of other things. And being distracted meant that she was succeeding here, in not having her life overtaken by melodrama and manufactured crises. "Life is not a made-for-TV movie" is the thing she kept reminding herself, also in Derek's voice. They had more important things to worry about, all of them. Her period would come eventually. Except it never did.

She couldn't say anything to Derek. He was still settling into his new role as party leader and his life was upside down. She wasn't so much coming second to his career, because second would be generous. Maybe there was a place for her in the twenty-fifth percentile? And maybe he wouldn't even believe her if she told him what was going on, because it seemed like ages since they'd slept together. There hadn't been any time to.

So Brooke did what women do in these situations, no matter how old they are: she called her best friend. Carly could have given Brooke a hard time about things, for her distance and the silences and how she'd acted like she hadn't needed her until there was no doubt that she really did. But Carly did not do this, because that's how friendships go, forgiveness being paramount. Brooke knew this now in a way she hadn't before, like how she also hadn't realized how wrong she could be, so convinced of the solidity of her perspective. Who needed friends, she'd asked, rhetorically, imagining that female friendships were just a hangover from adolescence, giggly girls in bathrooms, something that must necessarily be cast off on the road to maturity.

But they weren't giggling now, Carly and Brooke, as Brooke hovered over the toilet and tried to pee on a plastic stick, and Carly leaned against the door to keep any of Brooke's roommates from busting in, because the lock was broken, along with everything else in her crumbling life.

For the one hundredth time, Brooke said, "I don't even know why I'm bothering with this. It's a waste of money. I mean, it's barely possible. I don't know how. There's got to be some kind of explanation."

"But it's a possibility," said Carly. "I don't know why you waited so long."

Brooke finished peeing. Glamorously, she'd peed on her hands, and so she put the stick on the counter and washed her hands in the sink. They had to wait five minutes, the package said. Except the results were immediately apparent: the test was positive.

"Do we still have to wait?" she asked Carly. They were staring at the test, two pink lines side by side.

"I don't know," she said.

Brooke said, "Better be safe," and they kept watching, as though the results might change. As though they were watching something fascinating, and it was, in a way. Those two pink lines that had emerged in that white space like a scream, threatening to derail Brooke's entire life now—her job, her relationship, all she'd planned for herself and her future. This was a disaster, and such a confirmation of everything she'd suspected Derek really thought of her—that she wasn't mature enough to conduct a grown-up relationship—and her inability to handle all this would soon be apparent to everyone.

She started to cry. "I think this is it," she said, because they were thirty seconds away from five minutes, and the result was still the same. She'd gotten knocked up. She was an idiot. They could sit here for five minutes longer, and another five minutes after that, and this would still be what had happened.

Somebody tried to open the door. "It's occupied!" said Carly.

It was Brooke's roommate Bryce who called back, "Are there two of you in there? What are you doing?"

"We're fucking," said Carly. "Leave us alone." To Brooke, she said, "You really should get this door fixed."

"I think I really should just move out of here." And then it became overwhelming again. "But I don't know what I'm going to do now." Her plan, not that she'd ever admitted to it, had been that she'd end up moving into Derek's place. She spent so much of her time there anyway, which was why living with shitty roommates in a crappy house hadn't mattered to her so much. But now there was nowhere else to go, and they were stuck in the bathroom. And the test was still positive.

Carly said, "But let's not freak out. One way or another, we're going to sort this out." Brooke loved the way Carly said "we," as though Brooke wasn't alone in this, even though she'd never felt so all alone in her life, so lost and humiliated, and entirely steeped in shame. She was sitting on the toilet seat now, her pants back up. "Let's get out of here," said Carly.

Brooke gestured toward the test on the counter. "But what do we do with this?"

Carly grabbed the toilet paper roll and started wrapping the test around and around until it was unrecognizable, then she stuffed the bundle in her bag. It occurred to Brooke as she was watching her do this that it was the kindest thing, the grossest thing, that anyone had ever done for her. Then Carly took her hand and pulled her out into the sunshine.

As they walked down the street, Carly's arm around Brooke's shoulders, Brooke sputtered, "What am I gonna do? What am I gonna do?"

"The only way out is through," said Carly. "What do you *want* to do?"

"What do I want to do?" Brooke repeated. "I want to not even have this problem, is what I want. So, like, what I want is kind of beside the point here."

Carly stopped, and pulled Brooke around so she was facing her. She said, "But it's everything. What you want. You're steering the ship here."

Brooke said, "The ship has hit an iceberg."

"The damage is not irreparable," Carly said. "You're going to be okay."

Brooke said, "I don't even know." She sat down on the curb, and Carly sat down beside her.

"You don't have to figure it all out now. And you definitely don't have to figure it out alone," she said.

"Thank you," Brooke told her, but grudgingly.

Carly said, "I'm not talking about me. I mean, you didn't get yourself pregnant."

"Oh my *god*," said Brooke. Her head, her hands. "Do I have to tell him?"

"You don't have to do anything," said Carly. "But why wouldn't you?"

"Because of everything?" she said. "He's going to be furious."

"With who? With you?" Carly looked horrified, all her worst ideas about Derek about to be confirmed.

Brooke said, "Not like that. It's not him. It's just, he's so busy right now, and there's so much going on. He doesn't need this."

"Nobody needs this," said Carly. "But that's life. It's called taking responsibility for your actions. If the tables were turned—"

"But they wouldn't be," said Brooke. "With Derek, it's different."

"It's not," said Carly. "At least it shouldn't be."

"He wouldn't have let something like this happen," she told her.

"But guess what," said Carly. "He did. This is on him too."

"I'm so embarrassed," Brooke said. She started crying again, and it felt like she was turning circles, beginning the spiral down a drain. The ground underneath them was damp, and her jeans were getting wet. "This is such a disaster."

"Let's get up," Carly said. She pulled Brooke to her feet. "It's a start, I guess."

"Where are we going?" Brooke asked.

"We're walking," said Carly. "That's the point. Just keep on doing it. One foot in front of the other. Don't stop."

"Maybe I don't have to tell him," said Brooke. It would make things so much easier.

Carly said, "I think you should. You're not alone in this. You can't be—you need support. And he'll want to know. Wouldn't you?"

Brooke told her, "Honestly? Twenty minutes ago, I was completely in denial, and that was fantastic."

She went in to work that afternoon—Carly had urged her to take a full day off, but she'd only be sitting at home marinating in despair, and at work, at least, she could think of other things beyond her terrible fate. Plus, she'd texted Derek and asked him if they could get together that night, which wouldn't make any sense if she'd been out sick all day. He'd texted back right away, cheerfully enough, it seemed. He was in a good mood, which was fortunate, though she'd be putting an end to that soon enough. If, that is, she was really going to go through with telling him—the prospect seemed far-fetched still. How could such a thing occur? Any of it? And could she really get away with not telling him? Was that possible? Or even ethical? But then, how could he be angry at her for deciding not to ruin his day, his life? To throw a grenade right into the middle of their relationship. Who would ever object to missing out on that?

"Their relationship" made it difficult too, because it wasn't solid, this thing they had. It was still like walking on eggshells, or walking on sand, and maybe quicksand at that—all of those walks that weren't a saunter, a stroll. If Brooke had had a grasp on what they were together, it would have been that much easier to decide what was going to happen next, but the promises Derek made to her seemed different every day, subject to his various whims and fancies. She never knew what she was going to get.

"You okay?" asked Marijke, Derek's new chief of staff. Marijke had had her eye on Brooke, whom she'd usurped as highest-ranking woman in the office with her arrival, and Marijke liked to keep tabs on her as much as she liked to remind Brooke of her seniority. Sometimes Brooke convinced herself she was only imagining the tension between them, but other times it was undeniable. Marijke had caught her napping in the closet once, and now here was Brooke arriving at work midway through the day. The look on Marijke's face was disapproving, and for the first time it occurred to Brooke that her job may not be as secure as she'd taken it for granted to be. She had to get her act together.

She told Marijke, "I'm feeling okay." As far as everybody knew, she'd been under the weather for weeks, and while Marijke had urged her to take some time off to properly recover, she kept coming in. Late. She was a workaholic, was what she hoped they were all thinking, but it didn't seem like Marijke was buying it.

Derek was concerned for her too, she could see it, and she appreciated his attention when he came over to her desk. His hand on her shoulder—"Everything all right?" he asked. Her absence, the text—he was looking for her reassurance. She didn't usually ask for his time, because that was always a more difficult demand than it might seem, considering his schedule and how everybody wanted a piece of him. "You're coming back to my place tonight? We'll order pizza," he said. They had a standing order, extra-large Hawaiian with a side of wings. Anything that was *theirs* was especially precious to her.

He tiptoed around her for the rest of the day. She had made him nervous, she knew. He held her hand that evening when they left the office, never mind who was looking. Letting it go once they were out on the street, but their strides matched as they made their way to his building. He tried to act like nothing was up, talking about the day, someone's meltdown on Twitter. He'd be holed up in committee meetings all day tomorrow, but today had been a reprieve from the usual pressures.

He nudged her shoulder, "And now I get to go home with you."

She was quiet. They kept on walking.

He said, "What?"

"Nothing," she told him. "Let's just get back to your place." And because she hadn't assuaged his worries, what else could he do except walk faster?

"So we'll order the pizza?" he asked, once they were inside his unit. They'd been quiet in the elevator. It was crowded, and they'd stood on opposite sides, their usual routine, an attempt at being clandestine. He got off first when they arrived at his floor, and had started down the hall by the time she'd made her way through the doors.

"I guess," she told him, in response to the pizza.

He said, "You have to tell me what's going on."

She said, "Order the pizza." She was hungry. Lately she was always hungry, when she wasn't feeling sick. Could she drag this out and eat the pizza and delay delivering the news forever?

But no. She had to get it out there. She'd waited long enough, and Carly was right—he needed to know. Even more important—she needed him to know, even though she was afraid he'd be angry. But he'd be angry now if she didn't tell him. She was stressing him out, she knew.

"So there's this thing," she said, once the pizza was ordered. It would be at least forty minutes before the buzzer would ring and the delivery guy would arrive. Where would they be by then, she wondered? Would they even want the pizza after all?

There Derek was, expecting something, so she had to get the words out now, no turning back. Like a runaway train, just go. "And I'm totally going to deal with it. I mean, not 'deal with it' deal with it, or maybe. I don't know. It's all really messed up, and it's totally not your problem, but I needed to tell you. Or at least I think I do." Maybe she didn't? What if she held him here forever?

His eyes were locked on her, and never had he been so much in her thrall, she was thinking, as he kept waiting. But she could see it was fear, total panic in his eyes.

He was jumping ahead. "Has somebody been talking?" he asked her.

"What?"

He said, "Who knows?"

"Who knows what?"

He said, "What did you tell them?"

"No," she told him. "Just listen to me."

He stopped. "Okay." He still looked scared.

"I think," she said. "I'm pregnant." Those words. And they weren't supposed to be tentative, but if they were tentative, she considered as she was delivering them, it would soften the blow. But the words *I think* only made her sound stupid, she realized. Like someone who was dumb enough to get pregnant, like she didn't even know if she was or not. Simpering, *teenaged*, and she waited for his reaction, for the expression on his face to move from panic to terrified, but it didn't do that.

Instead, it was relief. "Oh," he said, the word drawn out long like a sigh. And then he reached for her and brought her into his arms, wrapping them tight around her, and it felt like she could breathe for the first time all day. Like someone had caught her now, and she was no longer in free fall. Every muscle had been clenched, but now the tension drained, and she just let herself fall into him, as though she'd been meant to land here all along.

They stayed like that for a long time, not saying a word. When she finally pulled away and looked back at his face, she could see from his expression that his thoughts were far away from there. He was calculating, all the wheels turning, columns lining up. He was going to deal with this. He was going to fix it. And she thought it might be possible that everything would be okay.

She asked him, "What did you think I was going to say?"

He said, "I don't know. Sorry, I'm jumpy. I'm paranoid. I was thinking this was something big."

She pulled away and looked up at him. "This *is* big."

"But this is us, you know? You had me thinking it was something menacing. Something outside that's beyond our control." There had been quiet rumors of dirty tricks, conspiracies to take him down since he'd won the leadership. Derek insisted he never listened to any of it, but Brooke knew it was getting to him.

She settled her head back against his chest, where she could listen to his heart's steady beat. She said, "I was afraid that you'd be angry at me."

He kissed her head. "No way," he said. "But yeah, it's a lot."

"I don't want to have a baby," she said, articulating this very solid fact for the first time, and it was a relief to say the words, to know she had a choice in the matter. She said it again, but with a caveat. "I don't want to have a baby right now."

Derek said, "No. Now is really not a good time." And she was imagining years down the line, after the next election. Maybe when his career in politics was done and he'd gone into something with a smaller scale. She still wanted to go back to school. She didn't want to have a baby until she was in her thirties, at least. There was all the time in the world—but still.

"I mean, if there was a way," she said. Entertaining the possibility, a sweet romantic fantasy. She had dreams about a future with Derek, about having a child together, but not like this. It would not be right now. There was no question. She leaned in close, and breathed him in. But suddenly he was sitting so stiffly beside her, differently, that it was hard to succumb.

She pulled away again. "What are you thinking?" She needed to know where this news had taken them, just where they were standing. Instead of answering, he pulled her back against him, kissing her hair, which didn't tell her either way.

When he finally answered, she was utterly unprepared for his words. "I'm thinking about you."

"Me?"

"Like, this *is* big. I didn't mean to imply it wasn't. Just taking a bit to process, you know. I mean, are you okay? How long—how long have you known?"

"I only found out this morning," she said. "Well, confirmed it, I guess. I haven't been feeling right for a while, but it could have been so many other things."

"But it wasn't."

"Not according to the test we did."

"We?"

"Carly."

"She knows?"

"I needed someone," said Brooke. "And you've been busy. I didn't want to bother you, just in case it turned out to be a false alarm."

"And you've been to a doctor?"

"Not yet.

"Just to be sure. I don't know—isn't that a thing people do?"

"I don't know what people do," she said. "I've never been here before."

He said, "Me neither."

"Really?" It was unusual, floundering into the wide unknown together. Usually Derek was the one with all the experience.

But he hadn't understood her. "What's that supposed to mean?" he asked.

"Nothing." He was struggling, mercurial. Usually he was the one she could count on to be steady. She took a deep breath to keep from crying. "Really, I didn't mean anything," she said. "I just think . . . that I need you to be careful with me right now."

"I am being careful," he said. But he wasn't. He was angry. He was being unfair.

She said, "And how am I supposed to know even? About everything that you've been through. Why should I just assume—"

"That I'm not the kind of guy with a pattern of getting girls pregnant?"

"You're twisting my point," she said. "I never said a pattern. But these things happen. They're happening now. I didn't know."

"Well, it's never happened to me before," he said. "What kind of person do you think I am?"

"It could happen to all kinds of people," she told him.

He said, "It's irresponsible."

"It was an accident," she said, now her turn on the defensive. "The pill. It's not a hundred percent reliable."

"I know," he said. "I don't mean you're irresponsible." He shook his head. "I mean, I *don't* know. I'm out of my depth here. I've got no idea."

"Me neither," she said, and she took his hand, and he held hers, squeezed it—and the relief at that. How incredible that it only took one person to make you feel you're not alone.

He was feeling it too, how much it meant, saying, "I'm going to take care of you. I believe in taking responsibility— you know that. That's what I'm telling you. So you don't have to carry all this alone. I'm right here," he said. Then he said it again: "I'm right here." Delivering her everything she'd wanted—in anticipating this moment, she would never have imagined joy.

They were quiet after that, until the buzzer sounded and the food arrived, and when he went to the door to get it he didn't even tell her to go wait around the corner. There she was on the sofa where anyone could see her, although nobody did because the delivery guy never looked up from his order.

Derek brought the boxes over and spread them out on the coffee table. "This is okay for you?" he asked. "The pizza?" As though she was particularly delicate, which he'd never treated her like before. She liked it, his solicitude, even though it made her uncomfortable too, because there was no room in Derek's life for a girlfriend who was a diva. If this was a test, she still had to play it cool.

She said, "Pizza's amazing," and took a bite to prove it, which was easy to do because she was famished. Together they ended up polishing off every morsel, sitting close together, and even though notifications kept arriving on his phone—she knew, because since they'd come home it had been buzzing—he never picked it up to check. Every single part of his attention was on her, and she felt stupid now that she'd even thought of not telling him, at how much she'd underestimated him, that she'd thought the burden would be hers alone.

Saturday, Later

Shondra Decker was right: Brooke was hard to track down. Do a search for her online, and you'll come up with a blonde high school social media star who lives in the Midwest and unboxes beauty products, and even if you drill down into the other Brooke Ellises who are less internet-famous, the only references you'll find to Brooke herself are from some old site that lists high school graduation dates, and an archived news article from an essay contest she won when she was seventeen. She had always been wary of putting too much of herself online. She had classmates who'd had full-scale mental breakdowns via video blog, and once that stuff is out there, there's no going back. When she began working in politics, she closed most of her accounts, and turned the remaining ones to super private, and even on those, she never posted much, using them mostly to keep up to date with friends and family.

So where had that photo in the newspaper come from? She wondered if Derek would assume she'd been the one to release it, along with everything else she'd blabbed to the reporter. Would he actually think she'd do something that dumb? Who else, she considered, had been cropped out of the shot? Whose birthday had it been, anyway? Examining her face and Derek's, their expressions—they looked like they were having fun, and anyone would think that they'd been good for each other, and there it was on the front page of the newspaper for the world to see.

Although—the photo was zoomed in so much to compensate for the cropping that the image was pixelated, and it was not a terrific shot of Derek, the angle emphasizing the lack of definition in his jawline. He wouldn't like that picture, Brooke knew, for many reasons. But would he remember that they'd been happy? It was only a little more than a year ago, which was hard to believe, and the night had been a good one. She could remember pieces of it. Those smiles hadn't been staged. She remembered Derek kissing her in the street at the end of the night, when going back to his place together was still a thing that was new and she thought they had a future.

DEREK MURDOCH'S GIRLFRIEND SAYS HE'S "ONE OF THE GOOD GUYS"

She read the headline again, and then sank down on the front steps to read the article. She wasn't ready to go back in, where her parents were up and waiting. Last night when she arrived on their doorstep, she'd given them the low-down: "Derek and I were involved, I'm sure you knew, and now there's going to be this story in the paper." And they'd been as unsurprised by the news as she'd been expecting, but they had questions. Were she and Derek still involved, and if not, why? And what did it mean to be "involved," exactly? Did this revelation have anything to do with the allegations he was facing right now?

They demanded: Had Derek hurt her? Why was she being implicated in this? Didn't newspaper reporters have anything better to do with their time?

Brooke felt now like maybe her parents even under-stood—the way allegations against Derek could have blown up like they did, how the press can make something out of nothing at all. "And I'm not even his girlfriend," she had to remind them, since they refused to grasp that part of the situation. They kept asking her, "Well then, why not?"

It turned out that there was nothing particularly damn-ing in the article. *Until recently*, it started, *Brooke Ellis, age 23, had worked as a political staffer in the office of Derek Murdoch, of whom rumors had been flying for years that he was prone to relationships with younger women who worked in his office.* They knew her major, and the year she'd graduated. That she'd started working in his office as a summer stu-dent, and how she'd worked for him for years after that. Their relationship was described as "on-again, off-again,"

and "sources said" she'd accompanied him on several official trips. And she considered again where the photo had
come from, from where Shondra Decker had received her
information. She wondered how much those sources really
knew, and how much they were actually saying.

Brooke was described as hardworking, cheerful, effective at her job, so it was unlikely to be Marijke the reporter
had been talking to. Well-liked, the article said, but in particular by Murdoch, who'd picked her out of the crowd as a
favorite quite early. And when reached, she had refrained
from comment except to say, "Derek was never anything
but a gentleman to me. He's one of the good guys. He's
one of the best guys."

The article went on to say that Brooke had left Derek's
office suddenly a few months ago, and moved back to
Lanark, where she had a job at the public library. And then
it went on to quote local real estate agent Jacqui Diamond
of Diamond Realty, the "top realtor in town" (who had
more guile than Brooke had given her credit for), described
as a close friend and former classmate. "She doesn't look
well these days," Jacqui had shared. "She looks like someone who's a bit haunted, to tell you the truth."

This part wasn't good, what with her being haunted,
and confirming all the rumors about Derek's proclivities.
"On-again, off-again," it said, which was a polite way of
saying that he was stringing her along. But it hadn't been
like that. Shondra Decker didn't get it at all, and Derek
would hate the article, all of it. Even the part where Brooke
said he'd never been anything but a gentleman. It was true

that with actual gentlemen, no one ever had to spell it out.

But the story also could have been so much worse. Brooke was relieved, and Derek should be too, although her parents would have no appreciation for this particular silver lining. They'd been worried about her already since she'd come back to town, hesitatingly providing the distance she'd been demanding of them so that she could be accountable to herself. But now they were going to think that she'd gone and messed up her whole life, and they weren't completely wrong.

In the street, a car slowed in front of the house, and the driver rolled down the window. Looking confused, he pulled over and got out. Brooke should have gone inside immediately, but wouldn't that only have made her look like she had something to hide? That this guy might have something on her, and all the power was his? It was first thing in the morning, and she was wearing pink pajamas left over from high school, her unbrushed hair like the worst kind of halo. There she was frozen, locked in his gaze as he walked up the driveway, arms swinging.

"You're Brooke Ellis?" he asked, confused, because surely he'd not been expecting it to be so easy to track her down, to find her waiting on the porch in her PJs. And she was so frozen that she couldn't even answer him. She didn't want to acknowledge he was there. "I'm Tom Payton, from the *Globe National*." The *Daily Observer*'s rival broadsheet— had he come all the way up here for this? "Nice morning," Tom Payton was saying. "I was wondering if you might be able to answer a few questions." He gestured toward the newspaper in her hands, the photo on the front page. "I assume you know what all this is about."

Suddenly Brooke found her voice enough to say one thing. "I have no comment." The she got up and brushed off her baggy pajama bottoms. The matching top had a pink kitten who was claiming not to do mornings. It was obvious why she hadn't brought these things to the city with her when she'd left home. Everything here that was hers were all the things she'd left behind.

Tom Payton was still talking, and so she said it again: "No comment." She couldn't even hear the words he said, just the sounds, the noise, he was making. That photo, that article, was going to be on doorsteps all over the country this morning, and the storm was just beginning—she couldn't let people see her like this. She didn't want people to see her at all, and so she went inside and shut the door.

Her mother was waiting. "Who's that?" she asked.

"A reporter," she said. "From the *Globe National*."

"And what did you say to him?"

"I said nothing."

"But he came all this way," she said, peering out the window, pulling the curtain aside.

"Are you serious?"

"I don't know," she said. "Maybe you want to deal with this. Set the record straight. The phone has started ringing too."

"Reporters?"

"No, but anyone we've ever known," she said. "They're all wondering if we've seen it." She gestured toward the paper in Brooke's hand. "Do I want to see it?"

Brooke said, "It's not that bad. I mean—" She showed her mom the photo where they looked happy. It could have been so much worse.

Her mom reached for the paper. "I'm going to read it," she said. "If everybody else is, I mean. I don't want to be the last one to know."

"There's not much to know. It's almost nothing." Brooke regretted keeping the relationship a secret from her family, and she knew this was the part of the story her parents would be disappointed in, the part of the story that would keep them from understanding that Derek had been good for her, that they'd been good together.

Tom Payton was knocking at the door. "Ignore it," Brooke said, and she handed her mom the paper. She should read it now and get it over with, like ripping off a Band-Aid. It had to happen, but even the idea made Brooke cringe. It was strange that her mother's learning the details of her adult life could make her feel like such a child.

But Brooke's mother was not considering the paper yet, too uncomfortable with ignoring the reporter. "Are you sure?" she asked. It was so contrary to her hospitable instincts, and what if the neighbors saw him out there knocking? There were two cars in the driveway—obviously someone was home.

"He certainly is determined," her mother said.

"It's his job to be," Brooke reminded her. "Don't worry about him. He's still being paid."

"You don't think it's a good idea to talk to him anyway?" she asked. "He might go away then."

"He won't," Brooke said. "He'll only attract others, like ants."

Eventually the knocking ceased, and then her dad went around the house and closed all the curtains. "How are you doing, kiddo?" he asked Brooke, which was his way of expressing concern. Neither of her parents knew what to do with her. They'd both read the article by now, but they hadn't said anything about it, and Brooke didn't know whether or not this was doing her a favor.

Her mother tried a different approach. "Derek never hurt you," she said. "Like they said—those girls—those things they said he did."

And Brooke said, "Oh, god, Mom," and she couldn't tell her anything. There was a distance between them that was impossible to bridge right now, except with her embarrassment. "It was really, really fine," she said. "He never hurt me. Not once." Or at least not in the ways her mother was supposing.

"I don't like the way he's left you so stranded, though," her mother said. "What happened there? Have you heard from him today? He had to have seen it."

"He probably has," Brooke agreed.

"But he's in town? This isn't fair to you. Couldn't he come over? If we're talking about gentlemen."

"It's really complicated."

"He gets a lot of leeway, your Derek," she told her. And privately, Brooke had to concede that this was true.

"It's not his fault," said Brooke. "And you like him. You've met him."

"But I never knew," her mother said, "what was going on between the two of you. Even though I knew there was something. He seemed nice enough, as your boss. I mean, I voted for the guy. But look at us now—we're barricaded in our house." Someone was knocking at the door again.

"That's not his fault," said Brooke.

Her mother said, "But it seems like nothing ever is." The knocking started up again, and they stood there, frozen, until it stopped. "The doorbell hasn't worked in years," she said. "It feels like a blessing now." Brooke followed her into the kitchen. "Have you eaten?" her mother asked. "You need to eat." Brooke's mom struggled with breakfast because soup wasn't much of an option, and while usually her fussing would have annoyed Brooke, at this moment it was welcome, such a mundane, ordinary thing. If a person was hungry, she ate, and Brooke loved that anything could be so simple.

But then they were distracted by a noise at the back door, through the laundry room just off the kitchen.

"Did you lock it?" Brooke's mom asked her father.

"I don't remember," he said. Did he really need to be so thorough? Maybe the whole family was overreacting?

Perhaps not, because then they heard the door opening, and footsteps, someone coming around the corner through the laundry room. But it was only Nicole, demanding, "What's going on here? I knocked and knocked, and no one answered. And the doorbell's still broken."

"Why were *you* knocking?" their mother asked. "We thought you were another reporter. You nearly gave me a heart attack."

"The front door's locked," said Nicole. "There were reporters here?"

"Just one, so far," said Brooke. "But it's still first thing in the morning. Better safe than sorry."

"So you're just going to keep hiding?"

"Name one good alternative to that," said Brooke.

Nicole had none to offer. "Just makes it seem like you have something to be ashamed of."

"They won't stop until I do," said Brooke. And now she was imagining herself hiding indoors for all of time, suffering the effects of vitamin-D deficiency. Was this her life now? She was supposed to go to work today, but she couldn't imagine sitting up there in front of the public, her own face on the newspaper front pages she'd have to hang up on the racks. Could she ever go anywhere again? She'd have to call in sick. Surely Morgan would understand.

"I can't believe you told them that," Nicole said.

"What?"

"That Derek was a gentleman? Give me strength. He doesn't need his ego fed."

"You knew about this?" asked her mother. "About the two of them?"

"I didn't know much," Nicole answered, "but enough to know she's being pretty generous there. What happened last night?" she asked Brooke.

"What about last night?" said her mother. And Nicole stopped. She'd said too much already.

"Nothing happened last night," Brooke told them. And everybody made dismissive sounds around her— Brooke had become an unreliable narrator. "Really," she said. "Nicole took me out to see Derek, and he'd found out about the article, and there wasn't much to say after that. So I came home. Here, I mean." Home was still her basement hole on the other side of town. Maybe she should go there.

"And he brought you back here," Nicole said.

"He got a friend to drive me," Brooke said. "He was in a difficult spot. If everyone knew I was out there, it would only make things worse." That was what he'd said.

"But if everyone was going to know already, why did it matter if you were there or not?" asked her mother. It was a question that had also occurred to Brooke, but then there were complicating factors in the situation her mother didn't know about.

"I think maybe he didn't want me there," Brooke admitted. She'd come here to escape from loneliness, but loneliness sounded kind of good at the moment, because her family had her cornered.

"I knew it," said Nicole, who wasn't helping. "You made me drop you off halfway up the driveway. I knew it didn't feel right. I knew I should have stayed."

"I wouldn't let you."

"So it's over between you and Derek?" her dad asked. "More 'off-again' than 'on-again,' I mean?" He was frying bacon at the stove now.

"I don't know where they got that," Brooke said. "We haven't been 'on' for a while. You probably guessed." They'd seen her sad and lonely all summer long.

"What happened?" asked her mother. She had even more questions after having read the article. "Is this what brought you home? Things went wrong between you? Because I never knew. It's made no sense. You'd been on this track so long and you were doing so well, and suddenly you're back and something's not right. Did he do something to you?"

Brooke said, "No. I already told you that." She had to check her tone—she sounded snappy. But she wished her mother would listen to what she was saying, instead of taking the story in all kinds of different directions. "Those women, I don't know what they're talking about. Maybe they were even set up, or they don't even know what they're talking about. It was a long time ago."

"So you're saying he's innocent," said Nicole.

"I think he is," Brooke insisted.

"Well, he's guilty of something," her mother said. "Because what's come over you, I've never seen anything like it. It's like someone put your light out."

Brooke said, "I don't know that that's a crime."

Her father cleared his throat conspicuously. "You might find some disagreement with that in this household."

Brooke said, "But I'm a grown woman." Except her tone had reached a hysterical pitch, and she couldn't have sounded more like a child. She took a deep breath to calm herself. "I just mean that you don't need to blame someone else. I knew what I was doing."

"But did you?" asked her mother. "He's so much older. He ought to have known better."

"But to say that," Brooke began, frustrated by the way they kept erasing her from her own story, "is to say that I didn't—know any better, I mean. You can't say I wasn't responsible."

"No one's saying anything," said Nicole. "But the dynamics are complicated here."

"I made my choices," Brooke said. "And I'm willing to deal with what comes from that."

"You mean hiding in the house with the curtains shut."

Brooke asked her, "What else can I do?"

Friday Night

"I told her that you were one of the good guys," she'd said to Derek the night before in his driveway, imagining she'd done something heroic, something he'd thank her for. She was helping, and she'd been so glad to be able to help, finally. So glad to see him there in the flesh, too, close enough for her to reach out and touch. She had been missing him in a terrible, primal way that she hadn't properly understood until now, when she didn't have to miss him anymore, a burden lifted. But also it felt like a dream, the kind you have when someone you've lost is standing before you, but as soon as you try to touch them you'll realize they're not really there at all.

And it was like that exactly, because he took a step back. "That reporter," he said, "she was writing about you." Which had never occurred to Brooke—she didn't know why. She just hadn't imagined herself important enough to be a character in this story, plus she'd done all the right things. She'd been quiet and discreet. But then, political scandals come like dominoes, one starts falling and then everything goes, and now it was their turn. Her turn.

"I didn't know," she said.

"You can see," he said, "how this makes everything really complicated. You just can't be here. Not right now, after this week, and everything."

She said, "I wanted to see you. I've missed you."

He said, "I've missed you too. But it's better this way. We agreed it had to be like that."

They had agreed, out of necessity, because of her pregnancy, but she'd thought it was just until everything had blown over. And while she knew it was better this way, the situation still came with loss and heartache, and all this time she'd been waiting for him to find his way back to her, but he'd been thinking they were done.

"Can't I even come in?" she asked him, desperate now. "Just to talk." She still felt tied to Derek, responsible for his well-being. And how do you go about undoing a knot like that? Was it really possible that she meant nothing to him, after all they'd been through? "Is somebody else here?" she looked up at the windows, at the warmth of the light that had drawn her in.

He said, "There's no one. It's not like that. I've just had this week—you've got no idea what it's been like."

She said, "I've been watching. Reading."

"You don't even know."

"You could tell me."

He said, "I can't." He pulled his phone out of his pocket. "I'm going to get you a ride." As though he could give her this one thing, like it was favor. But she didn't want it.

"Never mind," she said. "I'll walk." Because there wasn't a person she could call to pick her up in this entire town. She was so lonely. Derek had been the only thing keeping her from realizing how bad it had been all these months, but it had only been the idea of him, an illusion. The Derek in her mind bore very little relation to the Derek who stood before her now, this stranger who was refusing to touch her or even to listen to anything she had to say.

"Not a taxi," he said. It was humiliating. If she had to suffer this indignity, the very least he could do was drive her home, but he said he couldn't. "They know my car," he said. "Everyone's watching all the time now." So what? she thought. If he drove her home, they would be able to get right back to where they used to be, Derek in the driver's seat and her riding along beside him. Maybe then he'd remember how much sense they'd made together. If they got in the car, she could make him see. But perhaps he knew that, because he wasn't going to get in the car. He wasn't budging. "Besides, I've been drinking."

He started texting. And she felt so far away from him, like she didn't know him at all. It had only been a few months, but that time had changed everything.

"What are you doing?" she asked. Why couldn't he talk to her? They could sort this out together if he'd just give her the chance.

He said, "I'm texting Brent."

Brent, Derek's lackey. "What does Brent have to do with any of this?" And what kind of a solution was Brent going to propose to Derek's problem? Would he send in a bouncer and have Brooke thrown out over the fence?

"He'll get someone. Someone to drive you."

"I don't need someone. I'll walk," Brooke insisted. She really meant it, her restive legs that wanted now only to move. She even wanted to prove she'd walk, but she didn't have the courage to leave him behind just yet. She didn't want to accept that this was over.

He told her, "You can't walk." Still texting. "It's far, and dark and dangerous."

Brooke said, "Since when do you care what happens to me?"

"I care," he said. Looking up from his phone, finally—perhaps the tone of her voice was what had done it. His first strong reaction since she'd turned up at his place—he'd been keeping the lid on his panic until then. But this was a step too far. Because he did care. In his own way, detached, like she was a problem to be solved. Actual empathy, for him, might be too much to ask. Instead he took care, which was not the same as feeling.

She wanted him to feel.

But for him, it was about being *demonstrable*. Feelings weren't important. For him, it was about doing his own particular version of the right thing. It was paternal, awful, the way he insisted on staying out there with her while the minutes passed as they waited for Kirsti to arrive, even though she wished he would disappear, the only option if the earth was so unwilling to open up beneath her feet and swallow her. Derek's presence, which had always been so powerful—now it meant nothing. Worse than nothing. It felt like an assault, and she wondered how long this could go on. Was this torture? Such a silence, because he wasn't in the mood for small talk, though she wouldn't have been able to stand it if he were.

Finally she could see headlights coming down the road, and she decided to seize just one more opportunity to explain. As though the failure had been hers, and she needed him to absolve her.

"I thought if I could reach you," she told him. "If we could sit down and talk."

He said, "It's too late for that."

"For what?"

He said, "For everything."

She said, "I'm sorry," because it felt right, but it didn't sound right, once the words left her mouth. It was all so wrong. Her whole life had been in disgrace before his was, and he hadn't said sorry even once.

"DEREK MURDOCH'S GIRLFRIEND SAYS HE'S 'ONE OF THE GOOD GUYS'"

... ELLIS DID NOT RESPOND to follow-up messages asking for clarification and further details about the nature of her relationship with Murdoch.

The Observer has learned that she also accompanied him on several trips across the country, as well as to a handful of international destinations, which would be unusual for someone in the role of a junior staffer. It is unclear who paid for her travel, or whether her role on these trips was in a personal or professional capacity ...

Sunday Morning

That morning Brooke woke up in her own bed, back underground, her old familiar burrow. Never mind that it was in a room that still felt like someone else's, with its blank walls and the passing feet outside—at least it was at an address that wasn't listed in the phone book, where reporters couldn't find her and knock and knock and knock. Nicole had driven her back the night before after a long and surreal day at their parents' with the curtains drawn. To avoid the news, they'd turned off their phones and the radio and the television, playing board games, Clue and Boggle, and it felt more like her childhood than anything had in a decade, except that she and Nicole weren't dressed in matching pajamas, and also she hadn't been implicated in a sex scandal back then.

"You're not implicated," her family had insisted, fervently defending her honor and trying to carry on like everything was fine. Her dad had gone in to the restaurant that day, but stayed only an hour or so before leaving his assistant manager in charge because everybody kept hounding him. Her family knew the stakes now, that Brooke wasn't just blowing things out of proportion—but they also didn't understand just how wrapped up in it all she truly was.

"Those women," she told them, "his accusers—they're anonymous. So there aren't any photos of them to stick on the front page. They only have the ones of Derek looking guilty, but those are all used up now, so it's my turn—I'm a proxy. Which means that whoever sees my face after this is going to be thinking about whatever Derek was getting up to out by the garbage bins ten years ago."

"Which was nothing," my mother said. "That's what you said." She seemed desperate for this to be true.

And Derek blamed Brooke—that was the galling thing. The uncomfortable feeling she'd been sitting with all day, not even waiting for him to call anymore or having to pretend that she wasn't waiting, because she knew that it was never going to happen. The look on his face as she came up the driveway, and the way it made her feel: *besmirched*. She'd finally looked it up, "smirch,"—not online, because her phone was off, but in the dictionary on her mother's desk—and discovered the word meant "stained." Related words: disgrace, stigma, taint.

Standing there in the driveway on Friday, something had shifted in her, an awareness, but it was the kind of revelation that requires processing. So she'd let the feelings come on gradually as the hours unfolded after Brent Ames's sister dropped her off on her parents' doorstep, and it wasn't so long before it was hard to admit she hadn't always known it. Derek wasn't ever coming back, maybe she'd never even had him anyway, and everything she'd been holding out for was only an illusion. A delusion. She felt like a fool, but it would be more foolish to still be deluded, so there was that, even though this all meant that by Sunday morning she was drowning in a sea of despair—which is never a good idea for a person living in a basement.

The curtains were closed so she couldn't see the weather outside, or the footwear. It didn't matter, because she wasn't planning on going anywhere that day.

"You're really going to hide away from everyone forever?" her sister had asked the night before as they sat in her car in the driveway, engine idling. Brooke didn't want to get out because it was warm in the car and she could pretend it was the whole wide world. Nicole didn't want her to get out either, and had offered to take her back to her place and let her sleep in the spare room, to stay as long as she wanted. She promised to leave her alone there, give her space the way their parents never would be able to. But Brooke didn't want anyone's spare room, and Nicole's concern was as claustrophobic as their parents', and maybe worse, because Nicole could read her mind.

Brooke told her, "Maybe. I won't hide away forever, but definitely for the weekend at least. Until it all blows over." Lately a day or two was all it took before some other poor girl showed up on the front page of the paper in abject humiliation, somebody else's scandal. The newspapers in the library would be removed from the rod, and placed in a pile, and eventually in an archive. Her colleagues had seen that day's papers, though, and now she never wanted to see them again.

"You know we're on your side, right?" Nicole asked her. "I don't like this, how I just keep dropping you off in strange places. You don't have to do this alone."

"But I do," said Brooke. "You guys can only play Boggle and try to protect me for so long. Sooner or later, you're going to have to open the curtains."

Not today. Even though it would be harder for reporters to find her here, a person could theoretically kneel on the sidewalk and peek in the window and find her lying in this bed, four walls bare, the room mostly empty save for the bench press in the corner. She wasn't taking any chances. She could just imagine tomorrow's paper:

DEREK MURDOCH'S ON-AGAIN, OFF-AGAIN
GIRLFRIEND LIVES IN A DEPRESSING HOVEL:
SEE PAGE 3 FOR PHOTOS

And what if he saw it? She would be so embarrassed that this was her life.

She could hear Lauren in the kitchen, and decided to go find her. Sunday was the only day they both had off work, and while they usually spent it avoiding each other, today Brooke wanted company. The evening they'd been drunk together, just days before, had felt as low as things could go, but now Brooke looked back at it with nostalgia. How innocent she'd been at the time. What would she be looking back fondly on in a few days? What a week.

Lauren said, "I texted you—when you didn't come home. I was worried."

"I was staying at my parents'."

She said, "You never texted me back."

Brooke said, "I haven't been checking my phone." Her phone was just one more reminder of the outside world, and she didn't need it, especially when the only person she wanted to hear from was never going to call. She remembered the cocoon of her sister's car, the rain on the windows obscuring the view. How much she'd once taken anonymity for granted. Even when she and Derek were together, she hadn't properly understood what it meant, somebody always watching. She realized now why he'd required her to be so careful all the time, and what the stakes had been. She thought she'd understood before, but she hadn't. "Sorry to worry you." She hadn't thought about Lauren. If Lauren didn't come home one night, would she even notice? Were they at that point in their friendship? Did they have a friendship?

"I thought maybe you'd heard from him, your boyfriend."

"What?"

"When you didn't come home. That he was back in town."

"I don't think he's coming back," Brooke said. "You don't need to worry about that."

"I'm sorry," said Lauren.

Brooke said, "Coffee?"

"Help yourself," Lauren said with a shrug. The pot was full and waiting on the counter. Who knew they would be so compatible? And that it would be such a blessing to know somebody who never followed the news.

Brooke said, "Listen, if anyone comes around here—I'm not home, okay? Maybe I was never here in the first place."

"What's going on?"

"It's nothing," she said. "Just laying low."

"Are you in trouble?" Lauren asked. And it turned out Lauren had an imagination after all, because Brooke could see in her expression that she was thinking something terrible, maybe smuggling or murder. Lauren had no idea who Brooke was, so it really could be anything.

"I'm not in trouble," Brooke told her. "But you know how things are." And Lauren did know—Brooke knew that much from her history. Lauren's father killed himself when she was eight, and her mother lived in a care home because she suffered from early-onset dementia, and Lauren had learned much younger than Brooke of the bad news that can come from a knock on the door.

Lauren said, "I never answer the door. Nobody you ever want to see shows up that way. It's always salespeople, missionaries, or politicians."

Brooke said, "And politicians are the absolute worst."

BEFORE

After she told Derek about her pregnancy, his condo became her cocoon, and for two days Brooke lived inside it, finally yielding to her exhaustion and calling in sick to work. She reclined on his sofa, taking luxurious naps under a fur throw-blanket, naps scattered among bouts of mindless daytime television, comfortably dressed in one of Derek's T-shirts, all while he worked, because his was a life that couldn't be put on hold. But she could rest, finally. The next day she unearthed a bottle of lavender bubble bath from the collection of hotel shampoo bottles in his bathroom cupboard, and she took a bath twice, her first time in years soaking in a tub—an impossible dream in a shared house—releasing all the tension from her body. And there was food. After they'd finished their pizza the other night, he'd gone to the shop at the bottom of his building and come back with fruits and vegetables, organic apples and sugar snap peas, plus fancy crackers and cheese that cost more than what she earned in an hour. For the first time ever his fridge was full, and she helped herself, when she wasn't lying down warm and dozing. All her needs were taken care of, time was suspended, and she was taking notes, details for Carly, so she could tell her friend, *Hey, look at how you were wrong about him. Look at the way that he's been here for me. Let me tell you all that he has done.*

If she could have remained suspended, Brooke might have stayed in that place forever, where they didn't have to deal with anything, where Derek came and went and seemed happy to see her at the end of the day. He'd been worried about her, and was treating her carefully in a way he never had before—holding her close, touching her hand, kissing her head in the morning when he thought she was still sleeping. And she liked this, being cared for by him, the way he treated her tenderly. It made her wonder if it could always be like this—but then there were discussions they still had to have, decisions they would have to make. They weren't talking about anything right now, everything between them space and quiet. Their mutual agreement, unspoken, had been to make nothing irrevocable yet.

But the essential fact was that Brooke didn't want to be pregnant. She wished she'd never been pregnant, and no amount of comfort or tenderness was ever going to change that. Even the word "pregnant" filled her with such revulsion, all those ugly consonants, so if anyone had asked, she would have told them she was "knocked up," affecting a casualness toward the affair, all cool and breezy, the kind of person she wanted to be. But no one was asking, and she tried to maintain her composure, act her age, and not give Derek—when he was home—any reason to think that the terrible mistake he'd made in getting involved with her was any worse than he already thought it was.

Because he had made this mistake, they both had. Things were tender between them, but this was also what went unsaid during the comfortable and comforting two days that she spent ensconced in his world, in the evening when he came home, and in the mornings before she kissed him goodbye. They'd messed up, and that part was awful. She didn't want to be pregnant, and he didn't want it either. It was the only option. She wasn't going to have a baby.

"I don't want to have a baby," she'd said. And she meant it, except for the part of her—a part that was so minute she couldn't even properly call it hers, to claim it—that could consider something different. Maybe she was even waiting for it. For Derek to put his arms around her and begin a sentence with, "Unless . . ."

She might have been game for anything he'd suggested, especially under the spell of this cocoon, because while she didn't want to be pregnant, she did want a future with Derek, and what else was a baby but the future incarnate? She had a vision of a house, a kitchen window with sun pouring in around the curtains. Quiet, the way it had been the last two days in his condo, which felt like a home for the first time. And it would be theirs; all of it would be theirs, and so would the baby. And she wanted that. Because she wanted him.

But Derek didn't say "Unless." Those hours when he was actually around, he still didn't say very much at all. But he was with her now, Saturday morning, and he'd even skipped his run and stayed in bed beside her, his arms wrapped around her as the sun came up and light filled the room. And she was thinking, "Isn't this nice?" and "What if it could be like this?" She imagined that maybe he was thinking the same.

"I've cleared some space," he said, out of bed now and getting dressed. There'd been an event that morning, some kind of community fundraiser in a plaza parking lot, but he'd canceled his appearance, which was unprecedented. She was feeling special, wondering if there was enough food in the kitchen to conjure pancakes—did he even own a frying pan? She'd figure out something. But no. He said, "We're going out." Out for brunch, like regular people, pancakes and bacon, the greasy and substantial food that she was craving, and she wouldn't even have to cook it.

How long would this go on? she wondered, Derek delivering her everything she desired on a platter?

As she faced him across a table crowded with dirty plates, rinds and remnants—why hadn't the server come to clear the table?—she thought about how they were on the same page. "I just can't," she said, about a baby, but she wanted to explain that it wasn't a rejection of everything else—the cocoon, his comfort, the possibilities of their life together. Surely she could leave one and still keep the others? The last two days had left her feeling rather indulgent. "I just can't," she said again, for emphasis, to make up for the fact that she couldn't say what she just couldn't, sitting in the middle of a crowded restaurant as they were. But it was so noisy there that they could talk, albeit in vague terms, and no one would be able to overhear them. By the conspicuous way everyone had looked away when they'd come in, she knew that Derek had been recognized, but places like this were an ideal way for him to be in public, with a clientele too cool to be stirred by fame.

And now she was waiting for him to agree with her, to respond to her, for anything. Waiting for his *unless*, if he had one to give. But he was giving her nothing, barely looking in her direction, just over her shoulder, pulling his lips so very thin, a dead giveaway. Something was happening here. She said, "What?"

And he still didn't answer, wouldn't meet her eyes. So she implored him, "Say something. Please?"

This was the moment, she was thinking. If he was ever going to say "Unless." And this whole brunch was a gesture, and there was a ring in his pocket. Maybe he had planned it. What would she do if he asked her? Because maybe a ring wasn't even what she wanted after all, she was thinking, having not let herself consider how one thing might lead to another. But Derek was hard to say no to.

Except he wasn't even asking. He wasn't asking anything. What he finally said was, "Okay?" Not actually a question; noncommittal. His voice so low—he was used to speaking over crowds, not under them. Usually he dominated everything. Surely he had never been this quiet. Something had shifted, but what?

That morning she'd had a shower, blow-dried her hair, put on the only outfit she had with her—a T-shirt and yoga pants from her gym bag—but she'd washed it with his laundry. So she felt fresh, and now finally, they were having this conversation, after two days of being so careful, discussions of nothing of substance. Neither wanted to upset the other. And she'd been indulging in a fantasy that maybe this was what love was, fragile feelings hanging in the balance. But they couldn't hang there forever. She had to get an idea of what was going to happen. She'd thought she knew, but she didn't.

"I can't," she'd said, needing him to tell her that this was okay.

What he told her instead was, "It isn't up to me."

"But you're part of this," she said. "I want to know what you're thinking."

"I'm not sure you need to," he said.

And she didn't get it. "You mean, you want me to have it?" A baby.

He admitted, "No." Without explanation, or provisos. His answer was definitive, like a door slamming shut.

"So we are on the same page," said Brooke. At least there was that. Hardly the same as curtains in the window, but two people have to start somewhere.

"I just can't," he said.

"You can't," she said. Not understanding. "Can't what?"

"Go along with," he started. "Support. You know my feelings."

"I really don't," she said. "You're not even speaking in complete sentences."

He leaned across the table. "Termination," he whispered. Abortion was a word even uglier than "pregnancy." It sounded like "borstals" and "borscht," "divorce" and "abhorrent." The word was dangerous, and he wasn't even going to pick it up, was certainly not going to risk using it himself.

"But this," she said. "I mean, you and me—this is different." She knew his view on abortion, and even admired it, in a sense, though it also pushed her buttons. They'd argued about the issue, all the issues, on a regular basis, but she liked to think that they'd learned from each other, and she'd helped him write the very speeches in which he'd articulated his point of view. Respecting his honesty, and wishing nuance went down better with the public, but Derek was who he was, and it couldn't be helped. He wasn't like all the others with their talking points and appeals to the base. Derek was human, and difficult. It wasn't fashionable, but it was *real*, and people were craving realness at this moment of political plasticity.

But why didn't it feel real now, as she and Derek sat there together over main plates and side plates, the breakfast she'd devoured and that he'd barely touched, so close she could feel his knees knocking against hers, but with a distance between them that was insurmountable—had it been there all along? Why did it feel so wrong? None of it seemed real. She required love and comfort and arms firmly wrapped around her shoulders—right now, her appreciation for difficulty and nuance had evaporated. This crisis they'd found themselves inside was difficult enough and didn't need added complication.

He said, "I mean the things I say. You know that."

"But you don't want to have it either." Now she was pleading.

He closed his eyes and sighed, like all this was hard for him. "It's your choice," he said. "It's always been. I'm firm on that."

He was being so obtuse that it almost felt like a joke, a setup. She told him, "But that's like cheating. It just means you don't have to be responsible for what happens."

He said, "I *can't* be responsible for what happens."

"But not having it—that's what you want too." He'd never seen her cry before, in all these years, but tears were springing to her eyes now. She couldn't help it.

"What I want doesn't matter here," he said. "It's *your* choice." He was leaving her so lost and alone right now, turned around and around. Spinning. He was messing with her, like this was some rhetorical exercise, and now she was angry. Because this was her life.

"What if I had it, then?" she said. A threat. But he'd know she was bluffing, and she really was, because his refusal to be part of this, to support her, made the notion of a baby, of a future, just impossible. She could never have a baby with someone who'd done this to her, who'd left her so stranded across this impossible table. Any thoughts of curtains were a fantasy.

"Well, I guess that would be your choice," he said, that word "choice" again, like so many people in politics who'd turned choice into a weapon they would wield, and if Derek really believed she would make a different one, there would be fear in his eyes. But there was none. He knew he could get away with this. Of all the things Derek knew how to do, the most fundamental of them all was winning.

She said, "But this is about both of us." Her voice was shaky as she strung the words together.

He said, "I can't support this."

"It's what you want too."

"But it's not my choice," he said.

She said. "I need you."

He said again, "I can't." Then he looked around to see who might be watching them, seeing her crying. What had he imagined was going to happen, she wondered, as she blew her nose into a napkin? She didn't care who saw. "It's the principle," he said.

"And principles are what's important here?" What if he just couldn't hear how awful he sounded?

"Principles are always important. Without them, we're lost."

"Are you serious?" She was already lost, and she was watching him deliver those lines so smoothly, like a robot. But now she understood what people meant when they said they hated politicians, because that's who he was now— above it all, saying what he needed to say to keep out of trouble. To be unpindownable. The expression on his face was empty and unchanging—except she knew him well enough to know there was some strain there. To pull this off would be a feat of endurance, and he wasn't sure that he could do it, and she was torn between her impulse to give him what he needed, because that was always her instinct, and her fury at his refusal to acknowledge the complexity of the situation, the enormity of his betrayal.

She said to him now, not rhetorical at all, but with genuine curiosity: "Do you ever wonder what would happen if you just felt what you felt? Would the world explode? Would your head?" She wanted to know.

And it was like he hadn't heard her. Nothing.

She said, "What is happening?"

He said, "Listen, whatever you need—"

"I need you," she said. Some things were just that simple, or at least she needed him to be the person she'd imagined he was, which wasn't simple at all.

He said, "I can't."

"You're a coward," she said, not to be cruel, but because she'd just realized it and the realization was so incredible and out of the blue. A revelation. She'd never thought of it before, of how being principled was simply a matter of being above the fray, above the mess of it all, and deciding that the catastrophic state of the world simply didn't apply to you.

And he didn't even flinch, because she hadn't said it unkindly. He didn't deny it, either. He said nothing at all. Maybe he'd known all along, and sometimes wondered how he'd managed to fool everyone.

He said, "I didn't mean to." A tiny admission that he knew there was something wrong with this, with what he'd done. Was there shame?

She said, "Didn't meant to what?" She really had no idea.

He said, "It wasn't supposed to happen like this."

"But this is how it is." They sat there, the atmosphere between them so steeped with tension that Brooke was sure everyone around them could sense it. And between the two of them, who would yield first? But Brooke had a feeling. "So what happens now?"

He said, "I don't know," which was not the kind of thing he ever said, and the spaces between those three words were long and final, which made her understand that really he knew very well.

"You want to take a break from things?" Just articulating the idea made it seem impossible. Brooke was becoming detached from her whole life, like a shadow, and she imagined floating away, but no. There was no lightness. She was stuck here, immovable, locked in this moment.

"It's not what I want," said Derek. "But it might be for the best." And then it clicked, and she finally understood properly why he had brought her there, to this unlikely public place. It was a gesture, but not the one she'd supposed. He'd been certain that she would behave, that here, at least, she wouldn't make a scene. And for the most part, she had complied with that.

They were so far apart now, the table an impassable divide, and it seemed like a dream that she'd ever been close enough to touch him. That there had once been such a thing as intimacy between them. Was the story even true?

She considered just saying no to him. Refusal. She would not give in, and if he got up to go, she'd follow him. He couldn't shake her off that easily. She knew where he lived, where he worked. Would he call the police on her? Have her removed? And then what? Endless possibilities. Because she would never have envisioned this scene over brunch, how he'd twisted the truth with lofty ideas to create a reality in which what was happening to her had nothing to do with him at all.

"It's your choice," he kept saying. And it was. But she didn't want a slogan. She wanted to have a real conversation, one that mingled ideas in the same way they had joined their bodies, the messy miraculousness, the sweat and love. Or so she'd thought at the time.

And he was giving her none of it.

But of course, she wouldn't fight him. Refusal was a notion she might entertain, but it was outside her capabilities, which Derek knew even more than she did—otherwise, he never would have let her into his life, his home, his bed. He had always been good at knowing who he could count on—he prided himself on that.

So yes, the meal was over, and the server brought the bill, finally starting to clear the plates. Brooke pulled her wallet from her bag.

He said, "No, I'll get it," his hand on her arm to stop her, but she pushed him off. Not gently.

She said. "Don't." She didn't want his hands on her, trying to push her to do what he wanted her to. She pulled out cash.

"I'll get it," he said. Insisting, the way he always did, but it was different this time, and she wanted to be the one to insist harder, for him to give in to her for once, even though he didn't want her money, and he certainly didn't need it. But she forced it on him anyway, she paid that bill, and she put her coat on, while he looked around again to take note of who'd been observing this production.

He saw her watching and snapped back into character. He said, "Look, if there's anything I can do—" That insulting and ineffectual line that's really a polite way of saying, "Honestly, don't ever call me." Something you say at funerals to people you hardly know and don't really want to think about. In a conversation of startling cruelties, nothing else hurt her quite like that. And she could sense the distance, that she had just moved on from someone he'd hold to somebody he didn't touch anymore. No matter that right now inside her there was a part of him, the potential for a life. But to acknowledge this would be too difficult for his framework. He just couldn't. Her only choice was to go.

He hurried to put on his own jacket, and came rushing out of the restaurant after her, and she only stopped because she was still waiting for him to tell her he was sorry. That this whole thing was just a stupid mistake, and let's go home now. Which was why she endured his hug, so stiff and wrong, and it made her feel dirty in a way that their intimate encounters never had. The hug was too much, it wasn't real, and he didn't deserve it. She didn't want to give him the satisfaction of thinking this was okay, that things could be friendly between them. But she also had to let him have it, because sometimes it's easiest to take whatever little you're being offered. Besides, they'd still have to be friendly together at work when all this was done. She was only being pragmatic.

They lingered on the sidewalk. Nothing between them had been resolved, and she could tell he was uncomfortable with this, but his discomfort was giving her the smallest bit of satisfaction.

He said, "You understand the position I'm in." And Brooke stood there waiting, and listened, because she still was hoping he could say one more thing to make it all okay. But instead Derek was waiting for her permission to enact this heartbreaking, awful betrayal, abandonment. And she couldn't give it, because she could hardly breathe. If she started talking, she would never stop crying. "It's impossible," he said. "You get that, right?"

And she nodded. Because there she was in his gaze where she'd been a thousand times before, and when she was there, she would give him anything. It was the easiest thing just to be in his thrall, and she wanted to reach out and touch him, his face, his jaw. The scars on his neck and chest that he would have hid if he could, even though he'd lived with them on his body for thirty years. And she loved him with them, wholeheartedly. But it still wasn't enough.

He said, "Listen, if you need money, a ride somewhere. I don't know."

"A ride somewhere?" She didn't even know who he was.

He said, "I don't want you to think that I've just left you high and dry here."

"Haven't you?" What else was this? She'd never been higher or drier in her life.

He said, "I think maybe we just got in a little bit over our heads." Like this was just some sad and lamentable thing, and he'd already moved past it. Not even glancing over his shoulder. He would never look back.

She said, "You're really serious." It was incredible, the way he always managed to amaze her—but everything was different now.

He said, "What do you want me to say?" Which was his go-to calculation when dealing with most people, although he didn't usually say the words aloud.

Brooke said, "Do you really want to know?" He didn't answer. "I'll see you at work," she said, and started down the street. She didn't know if he watched her go, because she never turned around.

When Carly heard what had happened, she lost her mind, grabbed Brooke's phone, and dialed Derek's number, screaming obscenities down the line. And Brooke didn't even fight to get the phone back from her, because she thought he needed to hear all of it, and she didn't have the energy to stop her friend. Derek had always said that Carly was a bit much, and now he was finding out just how much. She hung up the phone, and Brooke asked, "What did he say?" And she told her the call had gone to voicemail.

"This is unbelievable," Carly said. "I thought he was a rat-bastard, but this is lower than my lowest expectation. That absolute shithead."

"But I get it," said Brooke. "Looking at it objectively. He's in an awkward place. I don't know what else he was supposed to do."

"Maybe anything?" she suggested, aghast. "Could he have done any less? Literally. He should be here for you."

"And he was," said Brooke, remembering those two days. "In his own way. This is complicated for him."

"It's more complicated for you," said Carly.

"But he's got his principles." Derek's arguments felt as ridiculous coming out of her mouth as they'd sounded coming out of his. "Maybe it's easier for those of us who don't have any."

Carly said, "Is there anything this guy has ever done that you can't misconstrue as noble?"

"It's not noble," said Brooke. "I never said it was noble."

"He's abandoned you."

"But he said to call if there is anything I need."

"Like what?"

"Like a drive."

"Like he's going to drive you?"

"Well, he can't," she said. "I mean, think about it. Derek Murdoch shows up at the abortion clinic. Guests have to sign in. They'd be all over him. A disaster."

"Might teach him not to be a hypocrite," said Carly.

"But he's not, see?" Brooke said. "That's the whole point. He refuses to be a hypocrite. He's very consistent."

"Which is the next best thing to being noble," said Carly. "What a catch."

"But I didn't catch him," said Brooke. "He got away, or at least I think he did."

"You mean he ran away," said Carly. "Because life got real, and Derek never knows how to handle that."

"I'm starting to think he was gone before it even started," Brooke said.

"You're lucky to be rid of him," Carly told her. "Dodged a bullet. You know that, right?"

But she really didn't. Days before, she'd had a boyfriend and dreams of a future, however far-fetched, and now all of it was quashed and she was pregnant, alone.

At least she had Carly, who came with her to the appointment and brought her back to her apartment in a taxi afterwards because her place was quieter and more comfortable than The Den of Debauchery, and Brooke curled up on her couch and Carly made her milkshakes and they watched an old movie they both loved, *The Legend of Billie Jean*. Carly's roommate had gone to stay at her girlfriend's, so it was just the two of them, and Brooke was taken care of, if not with fur throw-blankets. There had been plans for Brooke to get out of town that weekend and stay at a cottage with her parents and her sister, but with her giant sanitary-pad situation, hanging out on a dock didn't seem so tenable. She told her mother she was sick and stayed on at Carly's. Derek didn't call.

Three days after her abortion, when Brooke finally arrived back at her place, where she'd barely been for days and days, a giant bouquet of flowers was sitting on the porch. They were still wrapped in paper, but the flowers were definitively dead, all the petals shed, the stems turned to slime, and the whole package smelled like bog water. It must have been an impressive arrangement once upon a time, and she dug through the remains to unearth the card—*Thinking of you, Derek*. But of course she hadn't been home when it arrived, and none of her roommates had thought to bring it in, stepping over it every time they went in or out the door because they were accommodating people. Even if they'd brought the bouquet inside, Brooke didn't think they had a single vase in their household, or even an empty jam jar.

But it was the gesture that counted, so she texted him to say thank you. A secret text, because she'd promised Carly she wouldn't get in touch with him, or at least not unless he reached out to her first. But technically the flowers qualified as contact, though when her text yielded no response, she did her best not to be too hopeful after all.

She used up her vacation days, which had been accumulating for over a year now, three whole weeks, and the time off seemed like the healthy thing to do. Restorative. She expected to return to work afterwards like nothing had ever happened, because she didn't know what else to do with herself. This was her life. Naturally it had occurred to her that maybe it was time to look for another job, and Carly had been urging her in that direction since she resigned from their office years ago, but Brooke had no idea how to go about making the change. Working for Derek was the only career she'd ever had, except for slinging pizza. Starting over would mean going all the way back to the beginning, and she didn't want to do that.

But it would turn out that she wasn't actually running this show anyway, because on the morning she was due to arrive back at work, she got a call from Marijke, Derek's chief of staff, who asked if they could meet for coffee at a little place around the corner. Brooke had always found Marijke intimidating. Everybody did. Brought in to bolster the team after

Derek won the leadership, she was very good at her job, no detail ever escaping her. She was in command of everything, which Brooke had never appreciated enough until that morning. Marijke hugged her and asked her how she was doing, because that's the kind of thing people do, but her concern for Brooke's well-being wasn't the reason they were meeting now.

Marijke said, "Now, I realize this is a delicate situation." And of course she knew. Marijke Holloway knew everything. "And what you're going through, it's a personal matter. But a line has been crossed, I think. It just makes things very complicated. And so what I'd like to suggest is a different course of action."

"I want to come back to work," Brooke said, too force-fully, not understanding how things could proceed in any other fashion, because her job was her job, and she needed the connection to Derek, not at all ready to break it off just yet. The last three weeks without him had been difficult, such a void, and if he remained part of her life, she could make sense of their story. Declare that maybe it had meant something after all.

But Marijke said, "I'm not really sure that it's the best idea." And she went on about how Brooke had had a tough time, and maybe a fresh start would be the best for everyone.

"You're firing me," Brooke said, as the realization dawned. She'd seen it before, but never from this side of the table.

Marijke said, "No. Not at all. We've made a plan."

"We?"

"Derek and I."

"I want to talk to him," Brooke said.

Marijke said, "This was his idea." And then she hurried ahead, a torrent of words. "There's a plan," she said. "Hear me out."

Perhaps it would be temporary, she proposed, a break. But in the meantime, it seemed like the best course of action for Brooke to remove herself from the situation for a while. "The stakes are high," Marijke said. "And we can't have emotions running over at work. There is too much else to focus on."

She said, "There is an opportunity." A job, back in Lanark. Not at his local office, no, that was still too close. It was another position. "Derek pulled some strings, and they're basically offering it to you." The pay was not much lower than her job right now, but living expenses were so much lower outside of the city that it was basically a promotion. "I think this will be good for you," Marijke said. "It will give you some time and perspective, space. For both of you."

"This is Derek's plan?" Brooke asked. "To send me away?"

"It's not like that," she said. "But I do think it's the best thing to do going forward."

"And Derek does too?"

"It's all too much right now," she said. "For both of you. Working in the office, how are you going to move on?"

"He sent me flowers," said Brooke.

"I sent the flowers," said Marijke. She wasn't budging. This was happening. Brooke could rail against it, but all it meant was that she'd be stranded, unemployed. She'd become inconvenient and they were shipping her out of town. Everything she'd known about herself and her life had turned out to be wrong. "It's for the best," Marijke said. "I understand what you're going through and I know it's really hard, but you're going to recover from this. I promise, you will. But not if you stay here. It's going to take so much longer if you do, and it's not great for office morale."

"This is about office morale?"

"We don't need the drama," said Marijke.

"There won't be drama."

"There's always drama, Brooke," said Marijke. "This is not my first rodeo. It's why workplace relationships are advised against. You were told. It's in the employee code of conduct. And everybody always thinks that they're the exception, that it will be different this time." She said, "You've been lucky, really."

"Lucky?" Brooke would have laughed if there'd been anything funny about this.

Marijke said, "He cares about you. He does. He wants to make things right. We want to make sure you're okay, give you a rest from things. Which is above and beyond what's required. He wants to do the decent thing."

"I think it's too late for that."

"It is what it is," said Marijke, who saw the world as a series of contractual obligations. She had a legal background, and was adept at the small print, both reading it and writing it. She had Brooke here. "I can arrange for someone to clear out your desk," she said. "The library is flexible on the start date. They'll be emailing you a contract this morning." She was finished—her iced coffee was drained to the dregs and she'd folded her paper straw wrapper into a tiny cube. "The day is yours," she told Brooke. "Make the most of it." And then she got up and gave Brooke a quick hug around the shoulders, and left her there, heading on her way.

It felt like a show, her life then—though a show past closing night, and now the set was being dismantled all around her. The door and the walls and the entire horizon—pieces of plywood held up by jacks. She'd lost her boyfriend, her job, her social circle and her purpose, all alone now on an empty stage with all the lights off, and nobody was watching.

It was her last night in her room, everything packed up in boxes. Subletting had been easy—their house had a revolving door—but she was going to miss it here. It didn't seem properly real that she was leaving everything behind, and if she'd comprehended it properly, she probably wouldn't have been able to go.

"But you know that you don't have to," Carly had reminded her the week before. Carly was the only person who knew the whole story. She would have liked to invite Brooke to move to her place, to sleep on the couch even, except that she was just days away from leaving herself, departing for a six-month contract in Guatemala. Carly's room was packed up in boxes too, but she was actually excited about where she was going. "We could figure something out, though," she said. "You're not obligated to go where he sends you."

Brooke said, "But I don't know what else to do. And it's helpful, really, to have everything set." Derek and Marijke had made everything simple, and she felt too broken down to summon resistance, or to engineer her own way out of this trap. Her parents were confused by the new and mysterious developments in her life, by how little she was telling them about why her plans had changed—but they were hardly going to protest the good news that she was coming home.

She wasn't ready to be finished with Derek yet, and that was her secret shame. Even now that she'd seen who he was, and after what he'd done to her, when no self-respecting woman would have granted him her time, he was still on her mind. She had all the time in the world to miss him, and worry about him, feel responsible, even, for what she'd driven him to, because he wouldn't have liked the person he'd been that morning in the restaurant. Surely he wouldn't feel comfortable, either, leaving things between them as they were. She was still waiting for him to come in and save her, but maybe he already had?

Maybe it was for the best, was what she was thinking, everything that had happened, what they'd orchestrated: her soft landing, and a chance to get away. Maybe he knew what she needed right now, and she told him this in another secret text, though he'd never replied to the first one.

She'd written, *Thanks for everything—really. Job, etc. My dad's coming to pick me up tomorrow.*

Not expecting him to reply—or at least this is what she'd tell someone if they asked her, if she were forced to explain herself. Though this would be disingenuous, because of course, she *wanted* him to reply, but she was also sure he wouldn't—so wasn't it the same? It was almost like she hadn't texted him at all. Except, she knew, regardless of his response, if he got a text from her, at least she'd be on his mind. Maybe this was as close as it was possible for them to be right now. She didn't want to disappear from Derek's life or have him gone from hers, because it would mean that everything they'd been through had meant nothing at all.

His reply came hours later when she was sitting alone in her packed-up room, books in boxes, her bed disassembled. All she was left with was a mattress on the floor, and she was lying on it, scrolling on her phone, when the text came. Was it possible that her phone buzzed differently when she received a text from him? She'd always thought so.

Still at work, he'd written. Of course he was. *But not for long. Any chance I could see you before you go?* Upending everything, all the realities she'd convinced herself were no longer possible. She'd been just another girl, someone else for Marijke Holloway to take care of lest the office morale was disturbed.

But no, this was him right now, the impossible fact of his presence. He drove over to her place, and from her window she watched him pull up to the curb where a parking spot was waiting like fate. He came up the walk, and she heard the doorbell ring—a sound so ordinary. But this had never happened before. Derek had only ever been to her place a couple of times, and now she opened the door and there he was, hanging back like he didn't belong there, like he wasn't sure how she would receive him.

What if they were just two regular people who were meeting on a doorstep? Brooke could even trick herself into believing it was true.

"Hi," he said. "Can I come in?" He was sheepish, but then he often was. It allowed him to get away with things. She liked him so much better when he wasn't trying to be better than he really was.

She said "I guess," because "Why did you wait so long?" would have made the wrong impression, but there was no doubt that he knew what she meant. "My room's up here," Brooke said, as he followed her up the stairs and down the hall, because he didn't even know. He'd never belonged here, and had only ever left her at the door before.

But it wasn't her room anymore, bare, boxed-up, the walls blank except for the marks where the masking tape had been. He wouldn't get to see how she'd lived here, or to learn what this room could have told him about who she had been all these years while she'd been living in his world but he'd never ventured into hers. There weren't even curtains, although there never really had been. Years before, she'd tacked an orange sarong over the window that turned the whole room golden when the sun shone in, but now the window was naked, and the glare of the streetlight outside was cold and ugly.

"So, I guess you're really going," Derek said, eyeing the boxes, giving her mattress a kick.

"You didn't give me much of a choice."

He said, "How are you?" in that heavy, serious way that meant he thought he already knew the answer.

She said, "I'm okay." She was okay. She'd been telling herself as much for weeks, that she was okay, and she would get through this, and the focus should be on moving forward, one foot in front of the other.

Derek sat down in her desk chair and tried to spin it around, but stopped short because the chair didn't spin. Everything she owned was basically broken. "It's a shitty chair," she said.

He said, "No, it's good." There was nowhere else in the room to sit but on the mattress, and then he was looming huge above her. He said, "You're really doing all right?"

"Well, it's not exactly been great," Brooke told him.

He pushed off from the wall and rolled closer to her. She stared at his shoes. "You're pretty tough," he said.

She looked up at him. "You think?"

He sank down onto the mattress beside her, and put his arm around her shoulders. "And I've done nothing to make things easier. I know that." He pulled her close and kissed her hair, and she wondered if she'd conjured this, if it was possible to want something so badly that it arrived, but she was still too nervous to believe in it. If she dared to believe, would it just be snatched away?

She said, "This is confusing." She inched away from him. "I thought you needed distance. Marijke said."

He said, "But, I mean, that's just Marijke. It's business."

"She fired me."

"It's not like that."

"What's it like, then?"

He said, "Wasn't it all a bit much? And we had to dial it back from there."

"You and Marijke, you mean."

"It's the best thing for everyone."

"But I didn't even get to decide. And you didn't call, and now here you are. And I don't know what I'm supposed to do with that, where this is going."

"Could we just focus on right now?" he asked. "One thing at a time." He kissed her. And at first it felt familiar, achingly so, because it was, but it was also different than it had always been between them, when she'd been all too happy to have his kisses sweep her away. Because it is a fact that you should never kiss anyone who treats you badly. But what if this one kiss, she wondered, might be the one that brought him back to her? The kiss as conduit, and she'd always loved kissing Derek. She knew how to do that, but, as it always did between them, one thing led to another. For all his insistence on focusing on right now, he sure knew how to speed things along.

"Listen, I'm not sure about this," she told him. "And I'm bleeding. Still." Just a bit, but she wasn't comfortable.

He said, "I don't care about that. I want you." He said, "I've missed you." It had been just over two weeks since the procedure, which meant sex would be okay and unlikely to cause infection—she'd filed away that data at the clinic, not supposing it would apply to her. At least this time she'd be unlikely to get pregnant. Ha. But she also had a sanitary pad in her pants that was as big as a sailing ship.

And what would Carly say?

"See, I don't think so," Brooke said. She couldn't think of a single way in which this could end well, but then hadn't she known what would be the logical outcome when she agreed to have him come over? It was such a bad idea. But Derek had always been expert with the powers of persuasion, rhetorically and physically. His hands, the way he touched her body, which had felt so used up and wasted since all this had started. It had been dulled, she'd thought it was never going to want anything ever again, let alone be wanted.

"You're sure you're not into it?" he murmured into her neck. "Cuz, I don't think you're sure." And they knew each other so well, their bodies and their minds, and it was so easy just to follow him, to let everything else fall away, including her resistance. Carly was going to kill her, but maybe Brooke could have this one thing? These moments of comfort were all he had to give her, fragments, shards, but surely she needn't be deprived of everything.

"Come on," he said. "There you go," approvingly, as she let it all happen.

But it wasn't what she'd hoped it would be. There they were, but on a mattress on the floor with a bright light shining through the window that lit up everything. And she wished there was a way to turn out that light so she didn't have to see, to feel it all, because she was bleeding, sore and raw, and he didn't even seem to notice. And then it became a thing that had to be endured, because there comes a point when you've gone too far and there's no turning back.

She had to mop them up with towels afterwards, unpacking them from boxes, and Derek pretended not to notice the trouble, like the mess was nothing at all. Lying back with his arms around her, a single pillow between them to share, and all the discomfort seemed worth it when he finally said, "Tell me everything." So she did, about how nervous she'd been and scared, but the procedure had been underwhelming, anticlimactic. She couldn't believe that was all, this was it. She'd have to go to a clinic in a few weeks to have everything checked out, but basically they'd just sent her on her way.

"And you feel okay?"

"Except for the bleeding." And how she was weirdly emotional about the strangest things, and so many of her thoughts had been tied up with him. She'd thought he was angry at her. He'd left her all alone.

"It was clumsy," he said. "But I didn't know what else to do, and I got it wrong. And I'm sorry you had to go through it by yourself. I needed space to process it. It wasn't a situation I ever thought I'd find myself in." He held her closer. "I didn't know what to do." The bed was narrow, and the floor right there. Such a bright light, and she traced her hands along his body, the way she knew him inch by inch.

"I can't believe you're here," she said. She'd thought they would never be here again.

"You've been on my mind," he said. "You were always on my mind." The title of the least romantic song Brooke had ever heard, a song she'd listen to with her fingers crossed that whoever it was being sung to wasn't buying it at all, because how much less can you give anyone than that. But Derek didn't know that song, background music if he'd heard it ever.

"I wanted to see you," he said. "I didn't want you to go, and for us to leave it like that." She'd known he wouldn't. But this was not the same as him saying he didn't want her to go, so she said nothing.

Except for, "What is going to happen next?" Between them. Because this couldn't be the end either.

He said, "You'll go home. And there's a job there, and your family, and you'll wait for the pieces to settle. And it will be quiet, and a bit boring, but maybe that's what you need right now."

"How do you know what I need right now?" She leaned up on her elbows, and rested her chin on her hand.

"It's been a hard time," he said.

"Maybe I need you."

"I'm here," he said.

"I mean longer-term."

He said, "See, this is what I mean. You need something stable, and I can't right now. You know I can't."

"But you could." Pleading. She tried not to plead, but she'd been cool for so long, and here they were now, both of them, still smeared with her blood. They'd made something between them, but it was gone, and she wasn't ready to admit it yet. She couldn't. "Even though you can't. I know you can't."

He pulled her close, and she inhaled him, willing herself to remember what it was to be here. He said, "I've loved you, though. All along, I've loved you. I couldn't let you simply disappear."

But he did. And she understood, because that was what she always did. It was a lot to ask, a night on the floor on a mattress. He kissed her goodbye at the door, even though her roommate James was coming down the stairs and saw it all, which was complicated. He greeted James with "Hey" before James ducked into the kitchen.

And then it was as though it might never have happened, any of it. Except the next morning in the light of the day, which exposes details the blinding streetlights don't betray, once she'd stripped the sheets and realized the blood had stained the mattress, and no matter how much she scrubbed it remained. That mark, on the bed she would still sleep on, and it would still be there. Every time she changed the sheets, which was never often enough, but still, she kept trying to decipher what it all was supposed to mean.

Sunday Afternoon

Brooke had never been sorry for her abortion. She'd been sorry she'd ever become pregnant in the first place, of course, for the way it disrupted everything and how she'd been so drained of energy she'd feared never again making it through an entire day without collapsing. For a few weeks, she'd forgotten what it was not to be exhausted. What if this is me now? she thought, as she dragged her body through the hours when she really knew what was happening but still didn't want to admit it to herself. Tracing the downward spiral—is this how a person loses control of her narrative? Would it be possible to just go to sleep and wake up in a thousand years?

She couldn't envision any other possibility, but thankfully there was one, this procedure that would render her no longer pregnant, her life back on track. Unfathomable

mercy, abortion. It felt like a way out of this, without humiliation; necessary punishment for a woman stupid enough to
make such a mistake, to have fallen. To be smirched. This
was before she knew what was going to happen with Derek,
of course, who'd deliver his own humiliating punishment
along with Marijke, because Brooke had become a liability.
Although what Derek had delivered wasn't really about
her, Brooke knew. He'd been saving himself, trying to
avoid a moment just like this one.

She wouldn't make the papers for a second day, she knew.
They wouldn't be able to find another photograph, and if
they did, it would just show her probably wearing glasses,
hair that was more mousy than blonde. Brooke liked the
way she looked, but she'd always been an unlikely candi-
date for a sex scandal, and she would probably help Derek's
case more than harm it—sure he's dating younger women,
but if they look like a cross between your little sister and a
librarian, how bad could it be? This part of the story was
always going to be a stretch, and they were lucky they were
able to create an actual headline out of it. With Derek and
her bowling, which was so much more wholesome than
whatever he'd been getting up to out by the garbage cans.

Of course, there were other possibilities. She'd realized
all along that Derek was as terrified as she was of people
finding out about her pregnancy, the abortion. When he'd
seen that photo yesterday, the two of them "in happier
times," as they say, Brooke knew he was convinced the rest
would all come out. Or else he was afraid he'd left her so
unhinged that she'd want revenge, to run his holy name

through the mud. And certainly she had good reason to, at least according to Carly, who was also a liability.

"But why is he making it your burden that he's a hypocrite?" Carly had asked. She'd agreed to accompany Brooke to the clinic without missing a beat, but she still insisted on having her say. "He doesn't deserve you," Carly said. "Have I told you that?"

"You've told me," Brooke said—but what if Carly started telling everyone?

Though Carly wouldn't. Not just because she was far away in Guatemala—Brooke knew her friend would never betray her like that.

When Brooke went online, she saw that she'd been right; no one was talking about her anyway. Instead it was all opinion pieces and a tapestry of comments flowing after them—what a loss this was for progressives, they said. The party's real chance for a feminist leader was squandered, ironically, by allegations that he was a sex-pest. And the usual pontificating about you never can trust a male feminist anyway, because don't they always turn out to be the worst? How Derek had failed in his pledge to be all things to all people, which only proved it was time for the party to get back to ideological purity. Rumor was that Gordon Howland would be vying for the leadership at the forthcoming convention, hastily called. He hadn't been elected in fifteen years, but was coming out of retirement to remind everyone what the party's real values really were, to harken back to a time when men were men, and also gentlemen.

"Strong leadership is what we need now," people were saying, and also that the problem was too many folks today were all caught up in identity politics, which was another way of taking one's eye off the prize.

Brooke finally checked her messages after another day of avoiding them. The day before, her poor phone had vibrated right across the kitchen counter at her parents' place and fallen on the floor before she finally turned it off. When she turned it back on again, all the alerts were still waiting, from texts and emails, social media. Friends wanting to know if she was okay, people who weren't her friends asking the same question though she knew they didn't mean it. Other reporters who'd somehow tracked her down and wanted "just to talk." She had nothing to say in response to these messages, because it was over and Derek had dumped her, and she didn't want to have to break that story. There were limits to the humiliation one person was expected to suffer—or at least she hoped there were.

Outside her room, she could hear the television—a wall of sound, "Be My Baby" by the Ronettes—and she welcomed the distraction from the emotional demands of her phone. Lauren was still in her pajamas, curled up on the couch; the opening credits were showing for something.

"*Dirty Dancing*," she told her, as Brooke settled down on the couch's other end. "You like old movies."

"But I've never seen it," Brooke said. There was a terrible sequel set in Havana, and she saw that one at a party once. She did indeed like old movies, but this one had passed her by.

"It was my mom's favorite," said Lauren. "She watched it every time it rained, and I used to watch it with her, even though I only understood parts of it back then." She took a sip of her coffee. "Probably a good thing, too."

And Brooke started watching with her, a curly-haired girl in the car with her parents, an older sister. She's on vacation and not even unhappy about being stuck with her family, and her dad's that guy from *Law & Order* reruns. And it must be genetic, because the girl's got a thirst for justice, and social stratification at the resort they're staying at makes her feel uneasy. She insists on helping the bellboy carry the bags inside, and she's drawn to the resort staff, who are always dancing. Throughout her whole life Brooke had been hearing other people proclaim "I carried a watermelon," but she never understood what it was referencing. When the girl, who's called Baby, meets Johnny Castle, who's older and wiser than she is, they dance together, even though she's gawky and awkward. And then it turns out she's got something to teach him after all.

All this is a pretty predictable plot, but the part Brooke never saw coming: when Johnny's dance partner is crying in the kitchen because a waiter got her pregnant (the guy who tells Baby, "Some people count, and some people don't"), and they've got an appointment for her to have an abortion, but first they need to come up with the money.

Brooke had never seen an abortion in a movie before, and it was surprising to realize this because *Dirty Dancing* was over thirty years old. So it should have been a throw-back, but it was something very new: the character who *wants* an abortion. There is no other alternative, it doesn't even make her sad, and she doesn't change her mind at the last minute, or have a miscarriage as a convenient trick to avoid being an agent in her own destiny. She isn't sorry, either. Now they don't go as far as to actually say the word "abortion" in the film, but still. And then the procedure goes wrong, because this was 1962, when abortions were dangerous and illegal and the dancer, Penny, nearly dies. But Baby's dad is a doctor, and he saves her. They see her the day after in another off-the-shoulder blouse, and she tells Baby that she's going to be okay. She's even going to be able to have children one day—which is to say, she gets away with it. But Baby almost doesn't, because her dad finds out she's been sleeping with Johnny, and suddenly everything's shattered. Baby's dad tells her that she's not the person he thought she was—but then at the end of the movie, the triumph, he learns she's even *better* than he thought she was. Because it turns out she's a terrific dancer, but it's really her will he's admiring. And Penny who had the abortion is already dancing too—although that part, Brooke thought, was a little far-fetched. Her pants were *really* tight, which wouldn't have worked with the huge absorbent pad. But still, it seemed symbolic that no one had to live in shame. You could be a fallen woman, and then get up on a stage and dance. This was a huge revela-tion for Brooke, who had never even considered the pos-sibility, the number of ways a script could go.

She told Lauren as the credits rolled, "That is the best film with the worst title I've ever seen. I always thought it was supposed to be pornographic, or something."

"I love it," Lauren said. "It never fails me."

"Your mom had good taste," said Brooke.

Lauren said, "She really did."

"It must be hard," said Brooke. "With everything."

Lauren shrugged. "What can you do." It wasn't even a question. Lauren was somebody who'd never had a say in the defining events of her life. She said, "You just get on with it. You have to."

Brooke told her, "I got pregnant. In the spring." She wanted to tell someone. She was tired of this being her secret shame. It's when you can tell a story that you finally get to own it, rather than the story owning you.

But Lauren said, "What happened to the baby?" The baby. Brooke had never called it that. It had never been a baby to her, although correcting Lauren on this point felt awkward.

"Well, there isn't a baby." She would be six months pregnant now, she thought, surprised to realize that she'd been keeping track on a subconscious level. Imagining an alternative reality where she'd made another choice. A braver one, even? Although was there a choice in this scenario that did not require bravery? "Obviously."

She was waiting for Lauren to infer what had happened, because she didn't want to say the word. It was just the same as how they didn't say the word in the movie—but

Lauren just looked confused. She would have to spell it out. "The pregnancy. I had a termination. An abortion." It was really not such a scary word, and the meaning was dawning. Lauren got it, nodding. Brooke said, "Not like the movie. It's different now."

"The dirty knife and the folding table." A line from *Dirty Dancing*.

"It's different when it's legal," she said. "Clean." It had been.

"But your boyfriend," said Lauren. "Your ex. The rat. He broke up with you?"

"I think he did," said Brooke, and it felt good to say that. A line in the sand.

"That's awful," said Lauren.

"But maybe," said Brooke, "it helped clarify things. Otherwise he might still be stringing me along."

"And then you came back to town and moved in here. I knew there was something going on."

"Well, nothing's 'going on,'" she said.

Lauren said, "What are you waiting for?"

"What?"

"That's the thing. What I couldn't figure out, what you're doing here. What you're waiting for."

"I don't even know," said Brooke. "Maybe for all the broken pieces to be put back together again."

"Do you want to go out tonight?"

"Out?"

"What if we got dressed up and went dancing?"

"It's Sunday," Brooke reminded her.

Lauren said, "Half-price cover at Slappin' Nellie's."

It was a risky idea, she knew, going out and hitting the town. Maybe even just hands-down a bad one. Her face had been on the front page of the newspaper just the day before, and her emotional stability was fragile—she knew it was. She'd been through a lot. But staying home and hiding in her basement was an idea just as bad, and so was playing another round of Boggle with her dad in darkened rooms. There was not a single good idea among all her options, it seemed. There hadn't been in such a long time. And she was thinking of what Lauren had said: You've got to get on with it. You have to. So instead of waiting for something to happen, what if she made it so?

She knew what she was getting into. Half-price cover on Sunday nights is a Slappin' Nellie's special, and it's never crowded either, so that a high-profile local boy who's back in town just might decide to make an appearance. Even under the cloud of sexual misconduct allegations, because every local boy knows that his people are going to rally around him. Isn't this just what community is for? But even if Derek didn't show, Brooke wanted to be there. It wasn't all about him, and Brooke wasn't even fooling herself. She wanted to show her face, and drink and dance and have fun, and not be embarrassed about the recent history she'd been carrying around. The movie had been such a revelation. She hadn't done anything wrong, and she was tired of being punished—and why are only men ever entitled to feel so unashamed?

So they went. "I thought you were a nun," said Lauren on the way. They'd been drinking at home. After *Dirty Dancing*, they'd watched *Ghost*, because it turned out that Lauren's mom had been partial to Patrick Swayze in general. And then Lauren did Brooke's makeup, which she was very good at, and she had plans to do a program at the college, which was what she was saving her money for right now while her fiancé was out west.

She'd also loaned Brooke a sparkly tube top, which was too small for her, but Lauren said that only added to its appeal. They were both wearing tight jeans and strappy heels, and Lauren had magicianed Brooke's hair into an elaborate pile on top of her head.

"Well, I don't look like a nun now," she replied. She didn't look like the wholesome girl from the cover of yesterday's newspaper, either, and anonymity felt good. It had been a long time since she hadn't figured that everybody's eyes were on her.

Or at least if they had their eyes on her, it was for a different reason, she realized, when Brent Ames at the door didn't recognize her. She wasn't sure he'd ever looked at her properly anyway, just another one of Derek's girls.

"Ladies," he said as a greeting, as he took their cover and stamped their hands with red stars. Brooke followed Lauren into the darkness of the club's interior, the scene of so much youthful iniquity, where there had always been new shadows to hide in, new personas to try on.

They started dancing. It was the same music here that they'd been playing for years, and Brooke felt underage again, illicit. Eighteen and irresponsible, and she had another drink, the alcohol pulsing through her brain, making her head feel lighter and lighter.

"This was a very good idea after all," she yelled at Lauren, who was dancing in front of her, hands in the air.

"I told you," she said, and over her shoulder Brooke saw him, passing by the corridor on his way to the bar. Surrounded by his hometown entourage, all the guys he'd known forever. Her first instinct was to duck and hide, because he'd be angry if he saw her there. She was violating some part of the terms of their agreement.

But why was that even fair? she wondered. She had never agreed to anything. And who was he to tell her where she could and couldn't go, and she was so tired of taking instructions from Derek when he didn't even know what he was doing in his own life. So she kept dancing, and then Lauren led her over to two generic guys in Polo shirts.

"This is Rick and Rick," Lauren yelled.

"Which one's which?"

She said, "It doesn't matter." They all started dancing, and Brooke wasn't sure if Lauren knew these guys, or if she'd just found them, but maybe that didn't matter. And Rick and Rick gave her something to think about other than Derek, or at least something else to look like she was thinking about, because of course he was on her mind.

They were dancing to that old song "Two Princes," because half-price Sundays was also '90s night. And Brooke's

Rick was the taller one, grinding against her, both of them on display since the dance floor wasn't crowded. She had to look up to kiss him, her arms wrapped up high around his neck. She'd never been with anyone this tall before, and she was possibly even confessing this fact, her words slurred, in between wet kisses. And then she had a horrifying thought that maybe Rick was in high school.

"Are you in high school?" Brooke asked him. Why were the two Ricks dressed identically? Maybe it was a uniform?

But he was in college, he told her. In town for a volley-ball tournament, and when she asked him if everyone on the team was called Rick, he said no. His name was Kevin, and Lauren had been confused. The song changed, and they came apart, and Brooke could see Derek against the wall watching her.

She quickly looked away from him and kept dancing. Maybe she could carry on as though she hadn't noticed. She wondered what she'd looked like when she hadn't been aware he was watching her. What if he failed to recognize her just like Brent did? She imagined the whole thing coming full circle, Derek moseying on up to her, "Hey, you look familiar."

But Derek knew Brooke better than Brent did, and had managed to see through her brilliant disguise. He was coming over now with a puzzled look on his face. "What are you doing?"

"Hey, buddy," Rick/Kevin interjected.

But Derek ignored him. "What's this?" he asked, gesturing at her top, her hair.

"We came out dancing," Brooke said.

"We?" He thought Rick/Kevin and Brooke constituted a "we" now, and he was trying to make sense of all of this.

"Why's it any of your business?" she asked him.

Lauren was now standing beside her. "You know this guy?" she asked Brooke.

And Brooke said, "I don't think I ever did."

She was watching Brooke's face. "This is him?" she asked, and Brooke nodded. She turned to Derek and said, "You're an ass-hat. You realize that?"

"Who's she?" Derek asked.

Lauren answered, "I'm her friend."

Derek was pulling her away from them. "I have to talk to you."

Lauren was pulling her back. Rick/Kevin seemed to have disappeared to a place with less drama.

"We need to talk," he said again.

"That's not what you said at your house the other night," she told him.

"Leave her alone," said Lauren, still holding on. She whispered in Brooke's ear, "He's not even that cute. Are you sure?"

"This doesn't have anything to do with you," Derek told her. He looked at Brooke. "It's loud in here. Can we go someplace else?"

"Sorry, no," said Lauren. "We're dancing."

"I think Brooke can speak for herself," said Derek.

Lauren laughed, "Well, let's hear it then."

And Derek was pleading now. "Can't we go somewhere?

Just for a little while? And then you can come back to your friends." Brooke had never seen him so desperate, at least not since the press conference that had been the beginning of his undoing.

"I won't be long," she said to Lauren, and Derek led her out to the patio, which was empty tonight except for a few people who were smoking, and they moved past them. There they were, out by the garbage cans.

"There's some privacy here," he said.

"I've heard about that," said Brooke. "Your special spot. You've never brought me here before, though." Here it was, solidarity, long past the point where she should have recognized it. So she *was* the kind of woman who could end up out behind the garbage cans after all. Maybe every woman was that kind of woman, and it was knowing this that made a person truly responsible for her own life.

Derek said, "What's up with you tonight?" He even had the nerve to look hurt. He'd always claimed to like the way she gave it to him straight, but truth was she'd never given it to him straight. Not properly. "Your hair, those clothes?"

"What's it got to do with you?" she asked him. Truthfully, she was really cold.

"Because I care about you," he said. "And I've never seen you all done up like this. It's like you're somebody else."

"Still me," she said.

"Well, I hope so," he said. "But I just don't get it. What's going on? And with the reporter too, why you said what you said."

"You could have asked about it the other night," she told him, "but you didn't want to know." He had to know how much that had stung.

He said, "I'm sorry about that, about everything." There was a picnic table back there where the staff probably took their smoke breaks, a coffee tin for the butts, and he sank down onto a bench. The light was dim, but she could see that his face was tired. This week had done a number on him. "You said I was a gentleman," he said. He was staring at his feet. "It was not what I expected."

And probably not what she would say now, which is what she was thinking, in light of the last two days, but she didn't tell him this, because it was becoming obvious that Derek was in trouble. He was suffering. She asked him, "What were you expecting, then? What did you think I would tell the reporter?" She stared down at the top of his head, where the hair was beginning to thin. She'd never seen it before.

He took a breath, and exhaled with a puff of steam. The season was changing, and there was a chill in the air. She hugged herself to keep warm, and shivered, and he didn't even notice. "I don't know what I was expecting," he said. "I haven't exactly been stellar through any of this, I realize. Even before this week. And what you said, it was the first nice thing that anyone I really cared about had bothered to say about me since everything happened. I can't tell you what that means to me. With everything you could have said—you could have destroyed me if you wanted to. Even more, I mean. I wouldn't have blamed you."

"But I wouldn't do that," she told him. "Surely you know that."

"I don't know anything anymore," he said. "Not after this week. You think you have everything under control, and then it all comes crashing down. I didn't even see it coming. I mean, there were rumors, and other people weren't surprised. But I thought if I just kept my eye on the goal and focused, it would be okay. I never thought people would be this disloyal."

Brooke said, "So it's not true, what they're saying? Those girls?"

"It was years ago," he said. "I don't even know. I mean, of course not. Not the way they said it did. But sometimes things get misconstrued. How do you control the way that other people read things?"

"Read things like what?" This wasn't a literacy exercise.

"I don't even know," he said. "Ten years ago—it was another lifetime. And they're being put up to this—it's a political assassination more than anything else. In some ways, it's got nothing to do with the girls at all."

"Really."

"I don't mean it like that," he said. "But it's a setup."

"You know who they are, the women?"

"I think I do. Or I don't know. How do you ever know?"

"You mean because it could have been anyone?"

"No," he said. He was exhausted. "But it was such a long time ago. I don't even know who I was back then, let alone anyone else."

"So it could have happened."

"I was an idiot then," he said. "Still am, I guess. You know that better than anybody." He said, "Now I know how a downward spiral goes." Utterly defeated, and she was worried he was going to collapse entirely.

So she pulled his head against her chest, that tube top, which was nothing like her, but was something she could put on to become a person with the kind of nerve she dreamed of having. And she held him. Over and over, she'd think she'd never be able to hold him again, and then he'd be there right beside her, listening to her heart.

"I've done everything wrong by you," he said. "All of it—but especially the other night. You getting dropped off like that—how have you been living up here without a car?"

"I can't afford a car," she said.

"I should have thought of that," he said.

She said, "You don't have to think of everything."

"I was afraid," he said. "When I sent you away, and I didn't know what you'd told the reporter. It's been a terrifying week, Brooke. I don't know who to trust, or who's a friend, and I know I've been messing up you and me even longer. That I've let you down. But you're here. Even still, you're here. I don't deserve it. I don't deserve you."

And she knew he was right—he didn't deserve her. She didn't deserve any of the trouble he'd caused her in the past six months, her whole life turned inside out, but she kept coming back. She kept coming back for him, because it had to mean something, and if it didn't, then she really was a doormat, and he'd been wiping his feet all over her. He was doing it even now, but it still felt good just to have him there, to hold him. If she'd really been a doormat, would this have been the case? Only the two of them—the noise from the club seemed so far away. It was so easy just to believe in the two of them together. It always had been; reality was harder to fathom.

He said, "Maybe the only thing that ever mattered is you."

She tried to imagine what she'd advise a friend to do if she ever found herself in this place. What would her parents say, Nicole, Carly? Brent Ames's little sister? But what did any of them know about what it felt like to be singularly loved by Derek Murdoch, who'd had the eyes of the world upon him, but now only had eyes for her?

"They told me," he said. "Marijke and others, that you would be the problem. We had to get you out of the picture. Everyone was thinking about the damage you could do, but all along it was going to come from a different direction. And it was you all along, the last one left. Everyone else deserted me, but you're here, when you didn't have to be. When you had every reason on earth never to talk to me again.

"Do you know what it's like?" he asked her. "To have all the people you've ever counted on desert you when you need them most?"

She said, "To be honest, yes. It sounds a bit familiar."

"I'm sorry," he said. "I don't know that I'll ever be able to say that enough. I took the wrong advice from all the wrong people. I don't know what I was thinking, and I'm going to regret that for the rest of my life. I regret it more than I've regretted anything else, you know, and that's saying something. I should have followed my gut."

"Which was telling you what?"

"Well, to be with you," he said. "You're the realest thing I've ever had, and maybe I just had to lose everything else to see that."

She released him, and took a step backward.

"I messed up," he said, looking up at her. "I messed it all up, one thing after another. When I think about how alone you were and how I let you go in there and what happened to our baby."

"It wasn't a baby," she said, stopping him.

"It could have been." But it wasn't. That was the point, and it was up to her. "I just feel like I was given this chance, and then I threw it away." She couldn't argue with him there. "But maybe it's not too late."

"For what," she said. She took another step away from him.

"For us," he said. "For you, and me, and a baby. But we could do it right this time."

"Do it right." She couldn't imagine how he could expect her to think this was real.

Asking her, "Would you want to get married?" He shut his eyes and shook his head, saying, "I'm messing this up already. I don't even have a ring. I know there's supposed to be a process, but I didn't plan this. I never imagined that I'd be seeing you tonight."

He said, "Okay, maybe I should just stop now, while I'm still ahead. A little bit ahead. And I could go out and buy you a ring tomorrow. But if that happened, I mean. If I asked you what I asked you, what would you say?"

She said nothing.

He said, "Maybe there's a reason for everything. Maybe the baby was a sign."

"Of what?"

"Of other babies. You and me, I don't know. If we had a chance to do it again, we could make it all okay, what we did."

"What we did." But it could never be okay, not after everything. He really didn't see that. He was too busy talking.

"I've been thinking it through, and I've been thinking about atonement," he was saying. "If we could get it right, you know? It could make it all okay, what happened. There'd be a point to it all."

"It happened anyway," she said. "It's just that you weren't there."

"And I'm sorry." He got up from the bench and came over to hug her. "I'm so sorry. And I don't know what to do with that. How else to make it up to you."

"You want to marry me," she said. How could this ever have been what she wanted from him?

"It makes sense," he said.

"And would make things much more straightforward while you're facing allegations of sexual assault, I guess."

He said, "No. Come on now. It's not like that."

She said, "Isn't it?" She was freezing. He hadn't even thought to offer her his sweater, but instead he took her hand, held it.

"Would you marry me?" he asked her. "And you can pretend that I'm asking you this and we're the only two people in the world. That nothing in the last week, the last six months, has happened. Could we go back to the start? Would you forgive me for being too dumb to see what was right in front of me all along?"

There was just a single answer to his question. "No."

"What?"

"You heard me. No."

"WHO DARES TO PAVE THE ROAD FOR DEREK MURDOCH'S REDEMPTION?"

... WE'RE HEARING A LOT about victims these days, but who is going to be compassionate enough to think about the victims of these hate-mobs? Literally, this is a modern-day lynching, and these social justice warriors ought to be ashamed of themselves.

But ashamed they are not, not ever. Not even if photographs surface showing that accusers were dressed provocatively the night of the events in question, if witnesses attest that these women were so inebriated that one of them was found the next morning passed out in a puddle of her own urine. But I guess it goes to show that a person with no compunction about wetting her pants in public would probably not feel guilty about the opportunity to savage a good man's name, and leave his whole life in ruins. To hell with personal responsibility, I guess, and being accountable for our actions. Instead, let's just behave disgracefully in public and then ten years later come crying and blaming our bad behavior on somebody else.

And now what are we to do with Derek Murdoch, a man who has devoted the last fifteen years of his life to public service? While I was certainly never a fan of Murdoch's politics, it was undeniable that he was a person committed to helping people and making positive change. The loss of such a person in a position of leadership is a loss to us all, then, and one can't help thinking that the virtue signalers have come down even harder on him than they might have on their political opponents. Derek Murdoch's been made an example of, and now his former colleagues are wiping their hands of it all and feeling sanctimonious.

But they shouldn't be. What happened last week was even worse than a show trial, because there wasn't a trial at all. There was no due process. Instead it was all media spectacle, political theater. And now the show's over, and what's this latest flavor-of-the-week disgraced politician to do?

You might be thinking, "It's not my problem," but let me tell you that one day you'll be eating those words. And not even when it's eventually your own son, or husband, or father that they're coming for. No, even before that, before it gets so close to home. Because there are going to be all these broken, wounded men littering our land-scape, if things keep on as they have been. And you think that masculinity is "toxic" now? Well, get ready for a disaster when these men decide to rise back up and take what's rightfully theirs, what's been stolen from them. Once the feminists have spent all their outrage capital on microaggressions and manspreading, they'll be at pains to know how to deal with these men who've been the carnage of the social justice warrior movement. These women are creating monsters, is what I am saying, if they continue to bask in the humiliation of men whose only crime has been being born male in an age where being male is an unpopular and dangerous thing to be.

Monday Morning

When she implored him to come with her out of the cold, he wouldn't even look her way. He was humiliated, shrinking on a picnic bench, where it smelled like garbage and those cigarette butts in the coffee can mixed with rainwater. But she had to get out of there. She was freezing, and it turned out there was a reason that sleeves had been invented. She couldn't wait anymore.

"Come on, this is silly," she told him, one last try. If she could bring him inside, at least she'd know he'd be okay, that he wasn't just sitting out there falling apart, and she could pass him off to Brent or someone. Make him somebody else's problem. But he refused to budge, and she'd already given him enough, so she walked away from him. It was almost easy to do.

Back inside, she didn't see Lauren at first, although the

crowd had thinned out, but it wasn't long before she spotted her by the pool table, the Ricks now abandoned. She
wasn't dancing, and looked relieved when she saw Brooke.

"You're okay?" Lauren asked, trying to read her face to
discern the situation, but Brooke was confusing her. She
really was fine.

"We should get going," Brooke said. Even though part
of her wanted to linger, to see if he came in. But when he
did, what then? "We definitely need to go."

Lauren said, "What happened?"

Brooke said, "Nothing. It's really over now." She wasn't
even fooling herself, this finality she'd been craving. To
know what to do, even if it wasn't certain what was going
to happen after that. It was amazing even to know what
not to do too.

Eventually they found themselves in a taxi, and for the
first time in a long time she was sure of her destination.
They were going home. Lauren was quiet, and the driver
didn't make small talk either, because he could tell that
they were both beyond that. It had been a long night.

When they got back to their place, Brooke saw the
lights they'd left on in the windows, like a welcome, the
first time she'd ever felt genuinely glad to return here, but
maybe that feeling was also relief at knowing she'd be
moving on before too long.

"I'm really tired. Got to get some sleep," she told
Lauren when they got inside, and Lauren hugged her.
Brooke hugged her back, fiercely, and then she went into
the kitchen for a glass of water to help stave off a hangover,

turning off all the lights on her way back through. She took a moment to wash off her makeup in the bathroom after she'd brushed her teeth, the rare time she'd bothered, to get a glimpse of the person underneath it. She recognized that girl, and it felt like she owed her a few things.

There was a text from Derek in the morning, and seeing his name on the screen made her stomach drop. She thought she had expressed to him that she couldn't do this, keep being the one he crawled back to. He was having a hard time, but she'd had a hard time too, and she needed this break. She was sure she had been definitive for once, leaving no doubt in his mind. No "Maybe someday," the kind of thing she might have said before, infused with hope and faith—because she'd lost all hope and faith. Or rather, she'd decided to put her faith in different things.

But maybe he'd been listening to what she was telling him after all, because the message was something other than what she'd expected, not him begging for another chance. *Just one more thing, and I'll leave you alone*, he'd written. *I've got something for you, and it's at my parents' place. I think you know where that is.* How mysterious, and yes, Brooke knew where his parents lived. *My mother is expecting you.* Ann Murdoch, a pillar of the community, that force behind the organ.

Back in July, Derek's mom had been standing in line in front of Brooke at the grocery store, and she looked a lot like her son with her short no-nonsense hair and her compact frame, and it had felt incredible to Brooke that if she tapped this woman on the shoulder, she would have had no idea who Brooke was. She could tell her, "For about five minutes I was pregnant with your grandchild," and maybe she'd be destroying the world as Derek's mother knew it, or else she'd call the cops on her, another crazy lady in the grocery store.

But Derek's mom was expecting her now, and Brooke was due in to work at noon. There had been two days of newspapers since she'd been on the front page, but she wasn't sure it was safe to show her face around work yet. How long before she'd cease to be a public spectacle, and what would she do if she ever saw Jacqui Whynacht again? But, in the meantime, she'd go see Derek's mom. She'd get ready for the day and dress with more care than she would have on any other day, because it was her chance to make a first impression. But did it matter what Ann Murdoch thought of what she was wearing? What exactly did Ann Murdoch know about Brooke anyway, and also what had this dastardly week made of her? Would Brooke's arrival at the door be just one more thing for her, the final straw? Maybe the two of them would end up having a lot to talk about.

Lauren was still sleeping, so Brooke was quiet in the kitchen as she made her own coffee for a change, slopped some cereal and milk into a bowl. She ate her breakfast, and then got ready for the first ordinary day she'd had since everything had gone to pieces—but it was not altogether ordinary. Not with this mysterious errand.

What would be waiting for her, she wondered, making her way along the familiar sidewalks, seeing her shadow for the first time in days. There was sunshine, and the sky was blue, and it was the kind of weather that made you want to walk with purpose, even if Brooke didn't understand what her purpose was yet. It kind of felt like *The Wizard of Oz*, that this whole journey had been about arriving at what lay behind the great man—his mom? Who still drove around town in a minivan, even though she hadn't had to schlep anyone to soccer for years.

That van was in the driveway now, the house that little bungalow that had looked the same for decades, even while other houses on the street had had second storeys added, been torn down and then replaced with what passed for a McMansion in Lanark. A big picture window in the front, but the sun was shining off the glass, so it was impossible to see what was going on inside. Cement steps and a wrought iron railing up to the door, outdoor carpet on the porch with treads worn right through.

Brooke couldn't ring the doorbell—not yet. There was a quiet that she didn't want to disturb, nothing but the drip of water from the gutters. And on the other side of the minivan, she could see now from where she was standing on the porch: Derek's car, his SUV, yellow and shiny. So Derek was here. This was a trick. What had she gotten herself into?

Then the front door opened, and Brooke started at the surprise of it. And there she was before her, Derek's mom, half a head shorter than Brooke was, the expression on her face weary and hardened. Indeed, this had been a week, and she was like her house, weathered. Her youngest son had died, her eldest nearly killed in a fire at age eleven, and he would grow up to embody all her hope and dreams, until the last week had finally trounced them altogether.

She pushed the screen door open—"You're Brooke, right?" and Brooke said yes. Ann Murdoch didn't ask her in, but instead came outside wearing slippers, a hoodie with a high school crest that might have belonged to one of her children back in the day. Car keys in her hand. "This is a little bit irregular," she said.

Brooke asked her, "What is?"

And Ann Murdoch said, "What isn't? It's been a heck of a week." A point they could concur on. She said, "I read what you said about him in the paper. You were generous. He's been good to you?"

"He has been." There had been moments.

"He told me there's things he's got to make up to you."

"Maybe that's true too," said Brooke. "It's complicated."

"It's not that complicated," she said. "My son isn't always considerate. In general, yes, he cares about people a lot. But maybe not the particular ones. Not always. He doesn't see the trees for the forest, if you get what I mean.

She said, "He's had a hard time." And then she proceeded past Brooke down the steps from the porch, her slippers going slap-slap, and Brooke followed her. "Not that it's any excuse," she said. "I'm not making excuses, because there comes a point when a person knows what their lot is, and you've got to move forward with that. But

I'm his mother, you know. It's different. I was there and I saw it happen."

"The fire," said Brooke. They were standing in the driveway, and before them was a garage, but not the same garage, the one that had burned down twenty-eight years ago. The big aluminum door shut, and the van and Derek's car in the driveway before it. "Is he here?" Brooke asked.

"Is who where?"

"Derek," said Brooke. "His car is here."

"He went back to the city this morning," said his mother. "Someone picked him up—I don't know who. But he left the car for you."

"His car."

"He said you didn't have one," she said. "And he said there were places you needed to go, so the car is yours. He says he owes you." She was quiet for a moment. "And I suspect he does." She tossed the keys, and Brooke caught them, surprising herself.

"He gave me his car."

"There'll be paperwork," she said. "He'll have it taken care of." He really would. When Derek Murdoch did a thing, he always remembered the details.

"That's a pretty big deal," said Brooke.

"It's what he wanted," she shrugged. "And there's no telling Derek what to do. Maybe you know that."

"I do," Brooke said, and then she ran her hand over the hood, yellow paint sparkling in the sunshine. She didn't know what to say. If she just took this gift, what would Ann Murdoch think of her?

"Whatever he did, I'm sorry," Derek's mom told Brooke. And Brooke wondered if she thought Brooke was one of the women he'd taken out behind the garbage bins at Slappin' Nellie's.

"It wasn't like that," she told her. "Nothing so bad that I'd require his mother to apologize, I mean."

His mom said, "Mothers always end up doing the apologizing. So much so that their sons never notice they've done anything wrong." She was making Brooke uneasy, but didn't seem in a hurry to end this conversation either, slippers or no slippers. And Brooke could hardly just take off on her, having just been offered the gift of a car. Could she really just do that, get in the car and drive away like it was hers?

But in the meantime, she would have to stay here, have the conversation Ann Murdoch was itching to have.

"He's had a hard time, though," Brooke told his mom, echoing her words. Excusing Derek for the thousandth— last?—time. "With the fire." It was strange standing here in the place where it had happened.

"The fire," Derek's mom repeated, not looking at Brooke now, her thoughts carrying her away toward something else a long time ago. "You know about the fire?" she asked, returning to where they were. She gestured toward the garage.

"But that's a different garage."

"It was rebuilt," she said. "You might think nothing ever happened there."

"I know what happened," said Brooke. "Everyone knows." It had all been in the news long before she was born, but the legend had come down through the years. They'd reprinted newspaper headlines in his profiles, the pictures of Derek in the hospital wrapped up in bandages. Brooke hadn't been there, but she'd heard the story so often it was like she had been.

"He told you the story?" his mom asked.

Brooke said, "I know what everybody knows." She waited, but Derek's mom said nothing. Brooke said, "He saved them, his brother and his sisters. They were playing in there and something went wrong, lighter fluid or gasoline, and if it weren't for him, they could have been killed."

"If it wasn't for him," Ann Murdoch said, "it would never have started. No one talks about that."

No one did. "Did he really?"

She said, "Kids being kids. It happens. We should have done a better job keeping stuff locked up. I don't know where he got the matches. He never told me. He shouldn't get all the blame—he was only eleven. But I think about that, with everything that's gone on this week. I think about these stories we tell about people, but we leave out the details."

"He started the fire?"

She said, "I don't know. I shouldn't even be talking about this. I don't know why I want to. But it's just that people have been knocking on my door all week long, and you're the first person he said it was okay to open it to. I haven't been talking to anybody. We stayed home from church yesterday. I'm just exhausted."

"What happened?" Brooke asked, "with the fire?" Derek's mom wanted to talk. She seemed desperate, and Brooke felt as though she was being held hostage, and if she could just keep the woman talking, she would get out of this okay.

"The other kids weren't even in there," she told Brooke. "He was playing, and he started something going, and I don't think it was deliberate, and you know kids—they never understand the consequences of their actions. And then somehow the others were in there, and he was out here screaming, and I heard him. The phone was in the kitchen then, on the wall, and it was even before we had 911. I went to call the fire department, and I didn't understand. Why would the little kids be in the garage? There was nothing doing in the garage. They had a slide back there, and a sandbox, and it was a beautiful day. I thought the garage was on fire, and that was one thing, but I had no idea that my babies were in there."

"But he saved them," said Brooke. A prompt. That part, at least, had to be true.

And it was. "He went back in there," she told Brooke, "and came out with the girls, and I told him to stop, but he wouldn't. He had this coat, this green jacket, and he brought his brother out—Carl was still so small. And then his jacket had melted. I didn't understand that part either. I mean, the garage was on fire, but everything was fine, because there they were, one, two, three and four—and he was in shock, I think. And the whole coat had melted, third-degree burns. I didn't realize. He really looked fine, but there was this terrible smell, and it was the jacket and his skin, and then the fire department was there—it was only minutes, really. Everything was done, and then there was nothing else to do about it."

"Does he know?" Brooke asked her. "Maybe he doesn't. You know, the shock. He might not remember."

"He does," she told her. "And Carl knew. Carl heard me calling for him not to go back in there to save him. To save himself. A person doesn't get over that. I know he knows," she said, "because we had Carl to remind us. Carl never forgot."

She said, "He isn't perfect—my son. Derek isn't perfect. It's the thing they always say after someone does something reprehensible, isn't it? As though there was no other alternative but to be perfect, or to have done a bad, bad thing. If you can't be perfect, well then what's the point of even trying? But there are many degrees, aren't there, between perfection and being a sinner. And who among us hasn't sinned? It's the better question. But there are degrees there too. It's not all or nothing. And Derek had a hard time knowing that either way."

"He was a kid," said Brooke. Was it a sin to be a stupid kid playing with fire? Wasn't that a rite of passage instead? Most people just get to escape the terrible consequences. And Derek had always been drawn to extremes—all or nothing, indeed. Truly, his upbringing had not afforded him a great appreciation for nuance, and Brooke was sure the woman before her in slippers right now would be willing to take some responsibility for that.

"He does his best," Ann Murdoch told Brooke, looking just past her into a middle distance. "When he wants to, I mean. And then when he makes mistakes, he doesn't know how to take responsibility for them. He never did. We coddled him too much, because he was so hurt for so long, and because of the pain he went through. I couldn't be hard on him after that. Not after I'd seen what he'd had to suffer, and he had to live with what he'd done. Even after his body had healed, he was carrying that burden. He's tried to make up for it in every way, except for owning up to it. I'm not making excuses," she told Brooke. "It's just that these are the excuses I've got."

"You don't have to defend him to me," said Brooke.

Ann Murdoch said, "Oh, but I am sure I do." Then she checked herself. "You should go," she said.

"Where?" Brooke asked.

She answered, "That part is up to you." She gestured toward the keys in Brooke's hand. "He said you needed these."

"To get out of town?"

"To go where you want to go." Brooke clicked the fob and unlocked the door, and Derek's mom opened it up wide. "Get in," she said, and Brooke did, and then reached under to bring the seat forward and lock it into place. She knew this car, but had never sat on the driver's side.

She put the key in the ignition and turned the engine on.

"For real?" she asked Derek's mother again. All she had to do was put that car into reverse and back out in the street, and drive away. It was the first time Brooke could remember in such a long time with no limits. She could do whatever she wanted in the world.

Derek's mom shrugged. Despite the epic story she'd just told, the expression on her face had remained unchanging, matter-of-fact. She closed the car door gently, and then turned around and plodded back up the steps and into her house, closing the front door behind her without another glance.

And then it was just Brooke, and a car, and roads ribboning out in every imaginable direction from where she was idling now. She could choose any one of them, she realized. It was simply a matter of stepping on the pedal and deciding to go.

Or to stop.

Was it even as simple as that?

Because here was another option. Always, there would be other options. To turn off the ignition, get out, close the door. She could leave the keys in the mailbox, and set out on her very own steam.

Acknowledgments

Infinite gratitude to the booklovers—the heroic booksellers, avid readers, book bloggers, and bookstagrammers—who make my reading and writing life so much richer.

I am grateful to the amazing and inspiring Samantha Haywood for supporting my work and for finding it the perfect home at Doubleday Canada. To my editor, Bhavna Chauhan, from whom I have learned so much and whose excellent editorial suggestions brought my character to life—five minutes into our first conversation, I was already in love. Thanks to Melanie Little, Amy Black, Melanie Tutino, Terri Nimmo, Ruta Liormonas, and everyone at Doubleday Canada.

I am indebted to pop-duo Boy Meets Girl, whose catchy 1988 pop hit about unrequited love gave my book such a perfect title.

ACKNOWLEDGMENTS

Many thanks to the friends who celebrated the news of this book with me—Andrew Larsen, Denise Cruz, Krip Freitas, Nathalie Foy, Rebecca Rosenblum, Kate Wilcz (If I had a hammer?), Rebecca Dolgoy, Erin Smith, Kati Doering, Ann Douglas, May Friedman, Britt Leeking, and Jennie Weller. Thanks to Samantha Dempster for making everything gorgeous. Love to my Salonista pals. To Kiley Turner and Craig Riggs for my wonderful job at 49thShelf, deep in the world of Canadian books. To my coven— Karma Brown, Chantel Guertin, Kate Hilton, Elizabeth Renzetti, Jennifer Robson, Marissa Stapley—for casting great spells and being such excellent colleagues in the novel-writing trade.

I am grateful to my parents and sister for all their love and support, and to my children, Harriet and Iris, who always ask the most interesting questions and whose enthusiasm for books and reading matches mine. And finally, I owe everything to my husband, Stuart, who I was lucky to meet when I was twenty-three, who transformed my life into not just a love story, but also a grand adventure, and who once carried home a writing desk for me on his bike.